Conn... ...gh.
'It's o... ...Victoria,
that you're not too keen about
working with me.'

...e looked at her steadily. 'Perhaps you've
...ood reason… I know I was a brat at school.'

...ictoria was startled. That was something, she
...upposed—a kind of apology.

...t was a long time ago,' she murmured.

...is clear blue eyes held hers questioningly,
...nd Victoria suddenly felt rather flustered,
...s if a switch had been thrown to register a
...ixture of excitement and danger. She looked
...t him in confusion. She looked at his strong,
...telligent face and firm, uncompromising lips
...d swallowed hard. How extraordinary was
...at? She was beginning to admit to herself
...t she found Connor Saunders just as sexy
...w as she had when she was a schoolgirl!

Dear Reader

I am so thrilled that THE GP'S MARRIAGE WISH is being published in the Mills & Boon centenary year—it is such an exciting time, and I feel it is a real privilege to write for a great publishing empire and be a small part of its history. Happy Birthday, Mills & Boon, and may you continue to put romance to the fore for many, many years to come!

I love writing medical romances, and exploring the relationships that develop between patients and the people who care for them. The world of hospitals and surgeries provides a wonderful background for a romantic story between two people who love each other and have to deal with all the myriad dramas, both heartrending and humorous, that occur in the medical world. I really feel part of that world as I write and watch my characters unfold.

The idea of writing THE GP'S MARRIAGE WISH arose from meeting some old schoolfriends at a reunion, amongst whom was the drop-dead gorgeous boy (now a man!) we'd all fallen madly in love with in the sixth form! The last I saw of him at the reunion he was getting very friendly again with one of my contemporaries! Immediately the thought of Connor, my hero, sprang into my mind—the guy who'd been the centre of attention at school and, with maturity, was even more delectable many years later! In my imagination Victoria seemed just the girl to tame his macho manner when she re-enters his life!

I do hope you enjoy reading the story as much as I enjoyed writing it.

Best wishes

Judy

THE GP's MARRIAGE WISH

BY
JUDY CAMPBELL

MILLS & BOON®
Pure reading pleasure

All the characters in this book have no existence outside the imagination of the author, and have no relation whatsoever to anyone bearing the same name or names. They are not even distantly inspired by any individual known or unknown to the author, and all the incidents are pure invention.

First published in Great Britain 2008
Harlequin Mills & Boon Limited,
Eton House, 18-24 Paradise Road, Richmond, Surrey TW9 1SR

© Judy Campbell 2008

ISBN: 978 0 263·86343 7

Set in Times Roman 10½ on 12¾ pt
03-0808-51365

Printed and bound in Spain
by Litografia Rosés, S.A., Barcelona

THE GP's MARRIAGE WISH

Judy Campbell is from Cheshire. As a teenager she spent a great year at high school in Oregon, USA, as an exchange student. She has worked in a variety of jobs, including teaching young children, being a secretary and running a small family business. Her husband comes from a medical family, and one of their three grown-up children is a GP. Any spare time—when she's not writing romantic fiction—is spent playing golf, especially in the Highlands of Scotland.

Recent titles by the same author:

THE DOCTOR'S LONGED-FOR BRIDE

PROLOGUE

HE LOUNGED confidently against the wall in the assembly hall, a thick quiff of hair swept over cool dark blue eyes, watching the excited crowd of teenagers milling around him. Nobody could do attitude better than Connor Saunders—and he was arrogant enough to know that he made all the other youths at the Braithwaite Sixth Form College Ball look like wimps. He also had to be the hunkiest and sexiest guy in the room, thought Victoria Sorensen wistfully.

Victoria twitched her dress nervously and flicked a look at herself in the mirror next to the honours board—not a reassuring sight. She wasn't sure about the blue colour against her auburn hair, she felt her glasses made her look geekish and she was horribly aware of the wretched bands over her front teeth. If only she looked more sophisticated, stood out from the crowd a bit more, Connor just might ask her to dance... After today he was going to take a year out, going round the world, before studying medicine, and she'd be working at her mother's surgery before going to university, also to study medicine. She might never see him again.

A familiar mixture of resentment and jealousy jolted Victoria for a second—how easily everything came to Connor

Saunders! Girls, scholarships, medals—they all dropped into
his lap like ripe apples. There'd been an unspoken rivalry
between them for some time: she was just as bright as him,
but because he had the loudest voice, the cocksure personality
that almost assumed he would get every prize going, she was
left in the shadows.

A group of boys was round him now, laughing at something he'd said, and he was grinning back at them, flicking
back his hair, used to being the centre of attention. That was
the trouble, of course—he had such charisma. When he was
around there was a sense of fun and adventure—perhaps even
danger—and even though she resented the way he'd always
pipped her at the post in so many ways, of course Victoria had
been hopelessly attracted to him while they'd been students
together at sixth form college.

Her friend Jean Martin sidled up to her. 'Our hero's looking
good, isn't he?' She grinned, looking at Connor. 'And he
knows it,' she added.

'I can't believe I might not see him again for years…' said
Victoria bleakly.

''Course you will! Don't your mum and his dad work
together at the medical centre? There's bound to be occasions
you'll meet through them in the future.' Jean looked at
Victoria's gloomy face and sighed. 'Look, kiddo, you're mad
about him—why don't you ask him to dance before you go
your separate ways?'

'That's ridiculous—I don't want to demean myself by
pleading for a dance…'

Jean groaned. 'Come on, Vic, women have been emanci-
pated for nearly a century—why should we hang about
waiting for the men to get round to asking us? Don't be a

wimp—what have you got to lose? If you don't dance with him now, you'll never know what it's like to be held in those strong manly arms…'

An unwilling smile lifted Victoria's lips for a second. 'I'll just have to imagine it, then, I suppose…'

'Oh, to hell with it! This is your last chance. Go on, I dare you! He'll admire you for it!'

Victoria looked across at Connor doubtfully and just as she did so, their eyes met for a second, a flash of amusement flickering across his face as if he knew exactly what she thought of him. She flushed in embarrassment, then her mood became more combatant. Jean was right—why should she play the quiet little flower, frightened to approach him because of what he might think of her? Women didn't have to play a passive role nowadays.

She took a deep breath and walked up to him, ignoring the lads around him.

'Connor, I don't suppose we'll be seeing each other for a while. How about a dance before we go?'

Connor looked down at her lazily. 'Ah, Freckles…the last goodbye, eh?' He glanced around at his friends. 'Quite an honour to be asked to dance by the head girl, isn't it?' Then he lowered his voice slightly, his blue eyes dancing with laughter. 'It's been sparky competition between us for the last two years, Vic—I'll miss it.'

Victoria stood for a second, waiting for him to accept her invitation, and the little crowd around him watched them both with interest. Connor grinned at her, then nodded his head towards his friends. 'Sorry, darlin'—can't keep the lads waiting. We're off for a few beers before the pubs close, so the dance routine will have to wait for now. Some other time, eh?'

A ripple of laughter went round the boys and Connor lifted a careless hand to her and strolled out of the room, followed by his sniggering cohorts, leaving Victoria standing alone. She stared after them, her cheeks burning and a horrible suspicion of hot tears of humiliation in her eyes. It was as if she had been slapped in the face. How dared he embarrass her like that in front of everyone—how could he be so cruel?

In a second Jean was at her side, her arm round Victoria's shoulders. 'What a rat!' she whispered. 'Take no notice of him—that was all done to show off to that bunch of morons around him. Forget it ever happened.'

Victoria drew herself up with dignity, trying to disguise her bitter feeling of rejection, hardly able to believe that someone she'd thought had admired her, even though he might not have fancied her, could have snubbed her so publicly. Then that steely stubbornness of spirit that had rescued her so many times before when competing with Connor came to her rescue.

She turned with a bright smile to Jean, lifted her chin and said lightly, 'Manners maketh man… You're quite right, Jean. Connor Saunders is a complete rat and I don't care if I never see him again in my life.'

His tall figure disappeared out of the door, and despite her feisty words Victoria felt a hollow sense of betrayal. She'd been made a figure of fun—the girl who'd dared to ask Connor Saunders for a dance and been turned down for a few pints of beer! That was it, then. She would never think of the man again—from now on it was if he had never existed!

CHAPTER ONE

'VICTORIA CURTIS to see Dr Saunders, please.'

The receptionist looked over the counter at the tall girl with glossy auburn hair facing her, then peered at the screen of her computer, frowning slightly.

'You don't seem to have an appointment to see him. I'm afraid he's absolutely booked up this afternoon unless it's very urgent.'

Victoria smiled. 'But I'm not a patient—I'm joining the practice. I'm a doctor and he's expecting me.'

The receptionist's plump face looked startled. 'Oh. I'm sorry—I didn't realise there were two of you. Dr Saunders didn't mention anything.'

'Two of us?' questioned Victoria, puzzled. She had come to help her mother because Dr Saunders, the senior partner, was retiring and now she was here to go over some practice details, and her mother was joining them later. She wasn't aware that anyone else would be needed in the practice.

'I've probably got my wires crossed,' said the woman, smiling. 'I'll tell him you're here...' She pressed a switch. 'I've a Dr Curtis here to see you, Dr Saunders...'

'Ah—I'll be ready in one minute, if she could just take a seat in Reception,' said a deep male voice.

Morning surgery was evidently finished and Victoria sat waiting for him alone, sipping a cup of coffee that the receptionist brought for her. She looked around the room and smiled. It hadn't changed over the years—rather tatty-looking decor and a faded busily patterned carpet. Perhaps now she was going to be part of the practice, she could tactfully persuade her mother that the place needed a make-over.

She was sure her mother would be relieved that John Saunders was retiring. Victoria remembered him as an opinionated man, with a confidence that bordered on arrogance…very like his son, she thought suddenly. A picture flashed into her mind of the farewell sixth form dance all those years ago and the way Connor had made a fool of her. She hadn't thought about that episode for a long time, but she was surprised at how vividly the memory of her humiliation at his hands came flooding back to her—how it had shaken her confidence in herself for a long time.

Then she gave an inward shrug. No good thinking about that now. So much had happened to her in the intervening years, much worse than the teenage angst she'd suffered because of Connor. She'd been through a rough patch in the past year, but now for the first time in many months she felt excited and optimistic about the future—and it was lovely to be back in the beautiful Yorkshire Dales.

A few years ago she'd made a new life for herself in Australia, full of hopes and dreams that had been dashed, and the irony was that now she'd returned to Braithwaite again and put the fast-paced life she'd enjoyed in Sydney behind her to kick-start her life again.

'Dr Saunders asks if you'd go through to him now,' said

the receptionist, breaking into her thoughts. 'It's the room at the end of the corridor.'

Victoria made her way to the room, tapped at the door and walked in. A man was standing by the window against the light, and it was only as he strode forward to meet her that Victoria realised with a shock that it wasn't John Saunders at all. She gazed in astonishment at the broad-shouldered man who stood in front of her, looking as if he did a marathon workout daily in the gym, his body a sinewy combination of muscle and power, thick tousled fair hair flipping over blue eyes. It took her a second or two to recognise that he was Connor Saunders— no longer the lanky schoolboy she'd last seen at the leaving ball but a mature, eye-catching man with a commanding presence.

She drew in her breath, astonished at the coincidence that she'd only been thinking about him a few seconds before, the man who'd once humiliated her so cruelly in front of her friends. And like the automatic response of so long ago, for a split second she felt the faintest shiver of attraction flutter through her—an echo of what she had felt for him when they'd been teenagers.

'Wh-what on earth are you doing here?' she stuttered. 'I was expecting to see your father.'

There was surprise as well in the blue eyes that swept over her appraisingly, then Connor grinned. 'Well, well, well, I didn't realise that Freckles Sorensen had become Dr Curtis! We meet again after how many years?'

He held out his hand and shook hers. Victoria pulled herself together and removed her hand from his firm grip. She must have imagined that feeling of attraction a second ago—he was just an ordinary man who'd once been rude to her.

'Nobody calls me Freckles now,' she said coldly. 'Have you come back here for a holiday?'

'I've left the practice I was with in Glasgow and come to take over from my father,' he said simply, then raised a questioning eyebrow. 'And where have you come from?'

'I…I've been living in Australia…'

'Ah—you've come back to see your mother, then?'

Victoria gave a short laugh. 'Actually, I've come to help my mother in the practice because your father retires this week—I rather thought *I* was taking his place.' She looked at Connor in a puzzled way. 'What the hell's going on?'

'There's been a change of plan apparently,' he said laconically.

'What do you mean—a change of plan?'

He shrugged. 'Obviously I'm going to be working here as well.'

Victoria frowned. 'I don't understand… Mum never said she was taking on an extra doctor. When was it agreed that you should come?'

Connor sat on the edge of the desk, long legs crossed casually at the ankles. 'Only in the last day or two,' he admitted. He looked at her rather wryly. 'As a matter of fact, I'm as much in the dark as you are. Like you, I thought I was the only replacement.'

This is quite bizarre, thought Victoria crossly. Everyone seemed to have got their wires crossed. She hadn't come from Australia to end up working anywhere near Connor Saunders. Now she was standing opposite him the emotions he'd engendered that evening all those years ago came flooding back to her—the way she'd yearned to be in his arms, the pain she'd felt when he'd made fun of her. He was probably still as arrogant and insensitive as he had been then, and she would bet on it that he had never given a thought to that incident since it had happened.

She folded her arms and looked at him belligerently. 'I hope I haven't come all this way on a fool's errand—I was looking forward to working with my mother,' she said pointedly. 'I'd like an explanation as soon as possible.'

'So would I,' he agreed drily. 'They're both out on home visits now but I hope they'll be here soon to sort this out. I thought I'd be taking over from my father and then, when your mother retired, getting a junior partner in.'

There was the slightest emphasis on the word 'junior' as if to make it clear that he was ultimately going to be the senior partner, whoever he was working with. Victoria looked stonily at Connor—he might find that she had changed a lot since the days of Braithwaite Sixth Form College. What had happened to her in Australia had been horrible, made her doubt that she could trust any man again or feel that she could indeed be attractive to any other man. But it had also toughened her in many ways, and she wasn't about to be pushed around by anybody. She sat down by the desk and drummed her fingers impatiently on the surface.

'I suppose we'll have to wait until they come, then, for things to be clarified,' she said.

Connor flicked a look at her. Annoyance had made her cheeks quite pink, and her tawny eyes that had once been hidden behind spectacles seemed to reflect the colour of her glossy auburn hair. Victoria Sorensen had become quite a beauty since her school days—the unsophisticated teenager with the gauche manner had blossomed into a confident no-nonsense woman now, he thought with surprise. She'd been a bright girl at school—there'd been quite a lot of competition between them, and he remembered that he'd rather enjoyed stretching himself, always trying to outdo her in exams.

He had to admit he was quite shaken to meet her again. Perhaps deep down he still felt guilty about the way he'd treated her at that school dance—a picture of her stricken face as he'd refused to dance with her floated into his mind, and he recalled the inane laughter of the lads around him on the dance floor. He'd known he'd been cruel even as he'd done it, but he'd been an arrogant twerp then, enjoying the admiration of his mates at his rejection of Victoria, imagining what an alpha male it had made him seem. He felt contempt now for the youth he'd been and hoped against hope that Victoria would have forgotten all about it, although he suspected that she still remembered the incident. Perhaps that was why she so obviously didn't relish the idea of working with him.

Victoria was oblivious to his inspection as she pondered how unlike her mother it was not to mention that John's son was coming to work at The Cedars as well. If Victoria had known *that*, she wouldn't have come all these thousands of miles to work alongside a man she'd vowed never to speak to again! If only her travel arrangements hadn't gone so awry she'd have seen her mother the day before and perhaps all this could have been explained.

The sound of voices floated down the corridor, and then the door opened and Betty Sorensen and John Saunders came in. Betty ran over to Victoria and threw her arms round her daughter, hugging her tightly, then held her at arm's length as she looked lovingly at her.

'Vicky, darling! I'm so sorry I wasn't here to meet you. It's been such a hell of a week with one thing and another—and John and I have been run off our feet, dealing with the consequences of a gastrointestinal virus among the old folk.' She appraised her daughter beamingly. 'You look wonderful! I can't believe you're finally back in Yorkshire after five years…'

Victoria hugged her mother back—she had missed her so much over the past awful year when having her near to talk to would have been such a comfort.

'It's so good to see you, too, Mum. I'm sorry I couldn't get here last night, but with the plane so delayed I had to stay in London for the night and then get a train up here.'

'You must be absolutely jet-lagged, but never mind. You're here now…'

John Saunders stepped forward and took her hand. 'Welcome back, Victoria,' he said. 'I'm sure you've made a good move, coming back here.'

He was thinner than she remembered but nevertheless quite distinguished with a head of thick white hair and that air of slight self-satisfaction that she'd always found so irritating.

'Why don't we all sit down and have some coffee,' said Betty. She looked around at the others and smiled. 'We've so much to discuss…'

Victoria and Connor's eyes met for a second. 'So it would seem,' said Victoria lightly. 'I didn't realise that Connor would be working here as well.'

Betty gave a slightly embarrassed laugh. 'Well, things have been moving pretty fast here in the last week, haven't they, John?'

'They certainly have.' He smiled—rather smugly, Victoria thought. 'But now we can relax, knowing that you and Connor will be holding the fort!'

Connor looked from his father to Betty. 'I wish you'd tell us what you mean,' he said impatiently. 'Have both of us been offered jobs? And what's this about holding the fort?"

John gave a short chuckle and turned to Victoria's mother. 'Forget the coffee, Betty—lets get the bubbly out. We ought to toast Victoria's return—and we've got a little announcement to make ourselves.'

This is extraordinary, thought Victoria as her mother produced a bottle of champagne from a chiller bag. The pompous John Saunders seemed to be turning quite mellow in his old age—she never remembered him being so affable—and what on earth was he going to announce? She flicked a glance at Connor and wondered if he felt the sudden premonition of foreboding she was experiencing.

Betty handed round the glasses and John looked round at them all, raising his glass. 'I'm not going to beat about the bush,' he began 'The fact is, Betty and I have been working together for thirty years now and suddenly we've realised there's more to life than medicine…it's about time we had some fun.' He smiled broadly. 'We want to make up for lost time—and both being single and both realising that we've grown rather fond of each other, we've decided to get married and take off round the world when we've tied the knot!'

There was a stunned silence, the younger couple looking at their respective parents as incredulously as if they'd both divulged they were going to do a bungee-jump in tandem. At last Victoria managed to get out, 'You're getting *married*—after all this time?'

'And why not? Better late than never—the big day is this Friday. The practice—surely set in the most beautiful part of the country—is there for you two to take over immediately, with no strings attached! And we're starting on our cruise next week!'

'Next week?' squeaked Victoria. 'You can't throw us in at the deep end like that!'

'For heaven's sake, why the rush?' asked Connor, folding his arms and looking furiously at his father.

Betty stepped forward and took John's arm. 'I know this has come as a great shock to you both…'

'You can say that again,' muttered Connor.

'To be honest, at our age we may not have time on our side—that's why we want to get going. I know John didn't want me to mention this, but I feel you ought to know that he's been having treatment for Hodgkin's lymphoma…'

A shocked silence followed and then Connor gave a sharp intake of breath, looking stricken and concerned. 'Oh, Dad… why didn't you tell me?'

His father shook his head dismissively. 'I'm in remission now—and I feel fine, so we're seizing the moment, aren't we, Betty?'

'You should have let me know,' said Connor reproach-fully. 'I could have helped you out—taken time out from the job in Glasgow…'

John shook his head impatiently and put his arm round Betty. 'You've had your own problems, Connor. Frankly, my illness came as a wake-up call to us both—we realised how much we meant to each other and it was time to move in a different direction.'

Betty smiled at the two stunned people in front of her. 'You'll be fine, you know—it'll be a challenge. We know that both of you have had a rough time recently, and so we thought it was an ideal opportunity for you to make a fresh start—and help us out at the same time. I'm sure you'll work well together and bring fresh ideas into the practice. Frankly, it's beginning to get too much for me now.'

Victoria looked at her mother, whose cheeks were pink

with excitement, a kind of glow about her that made her seem almost girlish. Betty hadn't had much fun in her life—it had been all hard work and responsibility. Suddenly Victoria felt a wave of guilt when she thought how happily she'd taken off to Australia five years ago after her mother had seen her through medical school, leaving Betty to carry on by herself, her only child on the other side of the world. She couldn't spoil her mother's happiness by telling her that the thought of working with Connor was anathema to her and the fresh start she'd thought she was making in Braithwaite suddenly seemed a very unattractive prospect. She glanced at Connor's sombre expression. It was plain that his feelings mirrored hers, she thought wryly, but there didn't seem to be much choice but to get on with things. She swallowed hard and raised her glass towards the older couple.

'I'm sure we both wish you every happiness—and a wonderful and healthy retirement,' she said with forced enthusiasm.

'Of course,' added Connor. 'And we'll do our best to make sure The Cedars goes from strength to strength. It'll be quite like our old school days—working at the same projects. We should be used to each other's ways!'

Was that a broad hint that Connor expected to have the upper hand in their working life as he had done when they were students? Victoria took a deep sip of champagne and looked balefully at him over the rim of the glass—she wasn't going to let there be a rerun of their life at sixth form college. He might have a great physique and good looks, but if he thought he was going to get his own way when they worked together, he was in for a very nasty surprise!

CHAPTER TWO

'SO IT's all change, then, is it?' Karen Lightfoot, the practice nurse, stared with round, rather bulging eyes at Victoria and Connor. 'Talk about gob-smacked! I can't believe Betty and John are getting married after all these years! And now you two are taking over?' She shook her head dolefully. 'Any minute now I'll wake up and find it's been a dream.'

'As long as it's not a nightmare, Karen,' said Connor drily. 'We're going to try and make it work, but we can only do it with your, Maggie's and Pete's help. As a receptionist for some years, Maggie knows every patient in the practice, and although Pete's only been practice manager for a few months, I'm sure we'll be able to manage the finances as well as my father and Betty did.'

A week after her return to England, Victoria and the rest of the surgery staff were sitting in the office behind the frosted window of the reception area before surgery started. Betty and John had told them the week before of their departure and it was plain that they all felt as shocked as Victoria and Connor.

Victoria took a sip of strong black coffee, feeling rather like a condemned prisoner. The cold realisation that she was committed to share the running of The Cedars Medical Centre with someone she would never had chosen to work with was starting to sink in.

She looked across at Connor. She may have spent two years with him at school, but in many ways he felt like a stranger. She was still amazed that anyone could change so much physically—the callow youth with attitude had become a man with an air of authority about him, still undeniably attractive—but not to her, she thought fiercely. She'd learnt what he was really like—how could one feel anything kindly for someone like him? She bit her lip and doodled absently on a piece of paper. She was still raw from the sadness of breaking up with Andy so recently and that had made her more sensitive perhaps.

The thought of Andy reminded Victoria of the depressing news she'd received in the post that morning. It had been all she could do to force down a few cornflakes when she'd read it, reviving painful memories of her time in Australia. Its effect on her mood was going to make it a very long day indeed.

She was dragged back from her reverie to the present by the loud voice of Maggie Brown, the receptionist. She was a round-faced, pleasant woman with a wild bun of hair, which was escaping from numerous large hairpins.

'If we're making a fresh start, I want to put in a plea for another receptionist to help soon. I know we have Lucy, but she's only part time, and sometimes I'm run off my feet—I really do need some more backup. I've been telling John for ages that we're understaffed, but he never took any notice.' She gave a half-laugh to soften her words. 'If I have a break-down soon, don't say I didn't warn you.'

'We'll bear that in mind, Maggie,' said Connor gravely. 'Do you have any comments, Pete?'

Pete Becket, bespectacled and burly, nodded emphatically. 'We urgently need to run over the number of domiciliary visits and dermatology reports the practice has been racking up—we're going to be well over budget this year if we aren't careful. Of course it's been difficult to pin John down in the last few months,' he said, putting a large folder on the table. 'But we don't want to start off on the wrong foot.'

'And while we're on the subject,' broke in Karen, 'John did mention that we should think about getting a phlobotomy nurse—it would save so much time when we need blood samples, instead of sending patients all the way into Sethfield.'

'That's something that will have to be discussed with the other practices in our cluster,' said Pete. 'Now we're involved in practice-based commissioning it's important we put these points forward at the next meeting. And, of course, the biggest issue is the closure of the local community hospital, St Hilda's, to make way for commercial building in the town. Some of them are for it, others not.'

Connor and Victoria glanced at each other and he put up a hand. 'Hey! Give us a chance to take breath—we've only just got here! We'll certainly look into your concerns—I've been making notes so that Victoria and I can study them and then we'll have a proper meeting.'

'Asap, I hope,' said Maggie, 'otherwise I may come to a full stop!'

Karen stood up, her blue nurse's uniform straining over her plump body. 'Right—if that's all, I'd better get going and start doing the BP tests on the oldies now. I can hear the waiting room filling up.' She went to the door and then turned back to say brightly, 'Oh, and by the way, we need more coffee and biscuits, we're right out. Can someone get them before our break?'

'Well, I've no time to get any,' said Maggie firmly, as everyone began to leave the room. 'I'm just about to load the morning lists onto Connor and Victoria's computers—and I've got to switch the phones through now.'

Connor and Victoria were left alone. They stared bleakly at each other for a second as if the reality of working together had begun to sink in. Then Connor pulled forward the pad he'd been making notes on and said tersely, 'They don't seem very happy!'

'I'm afraid your father seems to have left a few problems behind him,' observed Victoria. 'As senior partner he had the final say in all the decisions. He should have ironed some of them out before asking us to take over.'

'Excuse me? What do you mean?' Connor frowned at her, his voice sharp. 'There were two of them here, you know. My father has probably been off work quite a bit with his treatment. Betty knew what the position was.'

'She was run off her feet—it's not easy to cope being the only GP in the practice,' Victoria pointed out forcefully. 'They should have got a locum in. It seems to me John was trying to save money.'

'That would have been a joint decision—and anyway perhaps some of things that have been mentioned aren't cost effective. No good splashing money around.'

He stood up and stared down at her frowningly, his eyes a steely blue. It made her feel a little…well, unsettled, as if he was looking right into her mind and didn't like what he saw there.

'I'm not blaming anyone—just stating facts,' she said.

'No, you're making suppositions, Victoria, jumping to conclusions about my father.' He glowered at her again, his strong face a study in anger. 'As I remember it from school, you do have a tendency to blurt out opinions without backing them up with evidence.'

Victoria laughed—it was such a preposterous statement. 'What the hell are you talking about? For goodness' sake, dragging up school days!' She looked at him scornfully. 'Perhaps it would be as well not to go back there.'

For a second he looked slightly abashed—perhaps he was remembering that night when he'd been so insulting to her, and she pressed home her point. 'To be honest, I don't know how we're going to work together if you're going to be so rude—in fact, I give our partnership a week or two at the most if this goes on.'

His strong face relaxed into a grin, making him look quite boyish, and he raised his hands in contrition. 'OK, OK, so I spoke slightly out of turn. But it's no good looking back at how the place was run and apportioning blame.'

Those blue eyes revealed a twinkle of laughter in them, holding Victoria's with a teasing charm, and to her continued annoyance she felt a treacherous and brief flicker of response to the sexy aura he exuded. Something about his eyes and the amused quirk of his mouth, she supposed. He had a point about looking back, though—the only way they could work together was to deal with the present problems and not point a finger at either John or Betty for causing them. Connor shot a look at his watch.

'Well, it's time to take the plunge now. We'd better thrash over these problems later—in the pub after work tonight suit you?'

Victoria shrugged unenthusiastically. She knew she wanted this particular day to finish early, to digest the news she'd received in the post that morning and wallow in a bit of nostalgia for things past. Discussing the troubles of the practice at the end of the day sounded very unappealing. 'OK, I suppose so…' She sighed.

'Don't sound so keen.' Connor put his hands on the desk and looked at her appraisingly with those startling blue eyes. 'Look, I can tell you aren't over the moon about working with me, but we've said we'll give it a go, so in the circumstances we'll have to make the best of things.'

'I agree with you,' she said coldly. 'We need to pull together to make a success of the practice, and I'm quite prepared to do that. I'll meet you tonight to discuss things, even though it's not actually very convenient.'

'Good,' he said briskly, gathering up some papers and making for the door. He looked back at her before he went out. 'By the way, if you need any help, let me know.'

Victoria's face burned with irritation. He might have been trying to be helpful, but she interpreted his offer as slightly patronising. She controlled her voice with an effort.

'I think I can manage quite well, thank you—after all, I'm just as experienced as you.'

He raised an eyebrow and gave a low chuckle. Victoria had become much more assertive than he remembered! 'Just a suggestion, Freckles—lighten up a bit. No need to be so deadly serious!'

He'd gone before she could think of a timely retort and indignantly she snatched up her bag. This was a fine start to the first day of work at The Cedars!

Her heart was thumping angrily as she stalked out and made her way to her room. She was cross with herself for allowing him to get under her skin—but she was a grown up now and in future she would maintain a dignified and professional approach, however much he irritated her, she told herself sternly.

Her first patient that morning was Janet Loxton, middle-aged and immaculately dressed in a tan suit with a black scarf draped elegantly round her neck. She sat down on the edge of the chair and Victoria took a deep breath and tried to calm down while she listened to the woman. Mrs Loxton's look was unnervingly hostile.

'I wanted to see your mother—she's my usual doctor,' was the unpromising start. 'I must say I'm shocked to hear she's left the practice.'

'She felt it was time to retire,' explained Victoria. 'She's now married to Dr Saunders and they plan to go away for a rest.'

'She might have given us more notice.' A deep sigh. 'Anyway, I suppose we'll have to get used to you.'

I seem to be surrounded by rude people, thought Victoria wryly, but she fixed a smile on her face and said soothingly, 'I'm sure when you get to know us better, things will be easier.'

Janet gave a cynical grunt, then said abruptly, 'I need sleeping pills. I'm awake all night and I'm run off my feet all day, looking after my father…'

Victoria groaned inwardly. It was Sod's Law that her first patient would start off with what she called a 'heart-sink consultation'. Giving sleeping tablets was something she was very reluctant to do, feeling it was a fob-off for a quick result, and didn't tackle the underlying causes—but in her experience the patient was usually adamant about having some!

'And is this insomnia something new?' asked Victoria.

'Oh, no, I've had it before. I suppose it's worry… Anyway,

you'll see that Dr Sorensen always gave me something for it. Just give me the same things, please.'

The woman's tone was peremptory, trying to hurry the consultation along. Victoria peered at the patient's notes on the computer and saw that her mother had indeed prescribed sleeping tablets in the past, but she was damned if she was going to just hand them out like sweets on demand.

'Do you work as well as look after your father?' she asked.

'I have a part-time job at the dress shop in the village. It saves my sanity. The rest of my time is spent running after an old man who needs professional help.'

'I take it he lives with you?'

'Yes…has done for the last five years. He needs to go in a home, though, but that's absolutely out as far as he's concerned.'

Victoria leant forward and looked at the woman sympathetically. 'It can't be an easy situation for you…'

'Of course it's not!' snapped Janet. For a second her mouth trembled, revealing very briefly the strain she was under. 'That's why I need these pills—I've got to get some rest.'

'Have you spoken to Social Services about getting help?'

Janet gave a humourless laugh. 'Oh, they've sent people in to give him baths, tidy him up a bit, but he's just sent them packing—he can be very rude when he wants to. Refuses to have anything to do with them. Do you wonder that I can't sleep?'

'Mrs Loxton,' said Victoria gently, 'you can't keep on these tablets for ever, and anyway the effect begins to wear off when you have them continually. You can develop a tolerance for them and need a higher dose to have the same effect.'

The patient leant forward and said intensely, 'I know all the pitfalls—you don't have to tell me. Your mother gave them to me, and I don't see why you just can't give me some without all these questions.'

'I can't just hand out prescriptions because my mother gave them to you,' said Victoria firmly. 'Your circumstances and health may have changed since you last saw her. However, I will give you a low dose of Triazolone—a ten-day course to try and get you back on an organised sleep pattern. But sleep disorders can be caused by a number of factors and I want you to try what we call sleep hygiene.'

Janet looked puzzled and Victoria smiled. 'Nothing to do with being clean! It's a kind of routine—wind down at the end of the day, don't stimulate your brain with television or exciting reading, and obviously cut out caffeine, and have a warm drink before you go to bed.'

'Yes, yes, I'll do all that,' said the woman impatiently.

Victoria looked at her patient reflectively. 'You know, what you could do with is some respite care for your father. Perhaps he'd be amenable to going into a home for a few days. It would give you a break.'

'I doubt he would—he's as stubborn as a mule. He's ninety-six and has always been like that, so I don't think he'll change now.'

'Why don't I come and see him and give him a general check-up? I could broach the subject to him then.'

Victoria printed off the prescription from the computer and gave it to Mrs Loxton, who put it in her handbag and rose from her chair.

'I don't think he'd want to see you—he doesn't hold with doctors and I don't want him upset because I have to deal with the consequences,' she said abruptly. 'Anyway, there's nothing wrong with him as far as I can see, except arthritis, poor eyesight and a beastly temper. Thank you for the prescription anyway.'

She disappeared and Victoria frowned as she updated the woman's notes. She wished she knew more of the background to Mrs Loxton's domestic affairs—was she married, and did she get any help for her father from her family? This was where her mother's knowledge would have been invaluable. She tapped her teeth with her pen thoughtfully, then pressed the intercom to the office.

'Maggie, could you spare a second?'

'Sure—I'll be with you in one second. I'm just sorting out some appointments.'

'I just need a bit of background information...I won't keep you.'

Maggie's face, surrounded by her wild hairstyle, peered round the door. 'How can I help?'

'I've just seen a patient called Janet Loxton—can you tell me her father's name?'

'Of course. He's Bernard Lamont. You may have heard of him.'

'The name sounds familiar—isn't he an artist?'

Maggie nodded. 'Oh, yes—he's one of Braithwaite's celebrities. He exhibits at the Royal Academy, I believe.'

'Ah, I knew you'd know about all the patients,' said Victoria. 'Can you tell me anything else about him?'

Maggie smiled—she looked quite pleased to be asked. 'He's a right curmudgeon, though of course he's very old now. I believe he can't paint any more, so that's hard for him. He and his daughter don't get on.'

'He lives with his daughter?'

Maggie nodded. 'Well, she moved into his house when her

marriage collapsed—that was a few years ago when Bernard Lamont was OK. Now she's got a new boyfriend and it can't be easy to carry on a romance with a demanding parent in the background.'

'Has she any family or siblings?'

'Not that I know of. She used to work in London when she was married.'

'Right. Thanks, Maggie, that's very helpful. It's good to get the background on patients' lives—gives me a fuller picture. I'll make a note to visit Mr Lamont.'

Maggie laughed. 'You'll be lucky—he won't see anyone.' She turned to go. 'I'll get back, then. Can't leave the desk too long at this time of day—it's like a jungle out there sometimes!'

They smiled at each other and Victoria pressed the intercom to summon the next patient with a sudden upsurge of spirits. She could see that Maggie had a sense of humour— someone she hoped she could have some fun with. Getting to know the patients and the day-to-day doctoring was part of being a GP, and if Maggie could help her fill in the backgrounds of these people, so much the better.

The morning spun by with a succession of patients with fairly mundane complaints from sore throats to bad backs, and by the time the last patient came in it was nearly eleven o'clock and Victoria could smell an enticing aroma of freshly brewed coffee drifting across from the little kitchen. She glanced at the clock— hopefully she'd be able to grab a cup in about five minutes.

A large, ruddy-faced man entered the room, leaning heavily on a stick, followed by an anxious-looking woman.

'Please, sit down, both of you.' Victoria smiled.

The man sat down heavily, his chest heaving in and out and a wheezing sound coming with every breath.

His wife started speaking quickly before he could say anything. 'I'm so glad we were given this appointment, Dr Curtis, because I'm really anxious about Dan. He's not been well for the last few weeks, but he wouldn't come and see you. Today he seems really ill, and I've said if he didn't come now, while he was in Braithwaite at the market, I'd throw his cigarettes away—and I meant it!'

Dan Wetherby shook his head, unable to speak, and Victoria got up and warmed her stethoscope in her hands. 'I think I'd better examine you, although I can hear your breathing's not good even before I look at you. Let's undo your shirt.'

'Susan's just fussing—there's nowt to worry about,' he wheezed, and was convulsed by a racking cough.

'I'm not fussing,' protested his wife. 'I knew your mother, Doctor—she's such a lovely woman—and she said months ago he was to come for a check-up. She even came round to see him, but he's that stubborn…'

Victoria waited until Dan stopped coughing and then put her stethoscope on his chest, front and back, listening intently. It sounded bad, as she had known it would, crackles and wheezes in all zones, and his heartbeat was very fast. The couple watched her face anxiously, trying to read from her expression what the diagnosis would be.

She put the stethoscope on the desk and folded her hands in front of her. 'You know yourself you've got a very bad chest, Mr Wetherby. How long have you been like this?'

'Weeks,' said his wife. 'I begged him to come and see you, but he wouldn't—the obstinate old fool.'

'Can't leave the farm,' wheezed Dan.

Victoria took a deep breath—she knew he wouldn't like what she was going to say next. 'You aren't well, Mr Wetherby,' she said gently. 'Your lungs aren't working as they should and I can hear all sorts of crackles. You need immediate hospitalisation to relieve your symptoms.'

'Can't you give me an antibiotic?' he whispered. 'That's what I had last time I had an infection.'

Victoria nodded. 'You certainly need antibiotics, but the hospital will give them intravenously to make them work more effectively, and in any case until you have a CT scan and a sputum test, we don't know exactly what we're dealing with…and we can't give you those procedures here.'

'I can't go to bloody hospital… I won't…'

Susan clasped her hands together and looked across at Victoria. 'It's bad, isn't it?' she said quietly.

'As I say, I can't tell exactly what's going on until tests have been done—and that has to be done quickly, and in hospital.'

Dan struck his stick on the floor. 'I'm not going—not without another opinion. Think of all the stuff I've got to do at the farm…'

Victoria looked at Dan's stubborn expression and sighed. Perhaps he felt he was giving in to his illness if he did what she advised. 'Look,' she said with an encouraging smile, 'what about if I asked Dr Saunders to look at you? If he confirms what I think, would you go then?'

'Might do,' he muttered.

'Oh, yes, you will, Dan Wetherby.' His wife looked at her husband fiercely. 'I'm not having another night like last night, with you hardly able to breathe for that cough. We'll see Dr Saunders as well, just to hammer home that he needs to go to hospital.'

'I won't be a minute, then. I'll just see if he's still here.'

Victoria went to the office to find out if Connor had started on his home visits or was still in surgery. He was sitting in front of the computer, peering earnestly at the screen and making notes.

'Connor, can I have a word?'

He swung round. 'Ah, Freckles…I mean Victoria. Don't tell me you need help already?'

Victoria looked at him coldly. 'Ha, ha. Very funny. Yes, I would like your help—and not because I don't know what's wrong with the patient,' she said defensively.

'I'm sure you do,' Connor remarked lightly.

She ignored his remark and continued. 'Mr Wetherby has chronic airway disease, very tachypnoeaic with widespread respiratory wheeze. I believe he should be admitted immediately for tests and therapy, but he's adamant he won't go until he has a second opinion, so…'

'You'd like me to come and look at him?'

'That's it.'

'Only too happy to oblige a colleague. Lead me to him.'

They went into Victoria's room and she introduced Connor to the anxious-looking couple. 'Dr Saunders will examine you, Mr Wetherby, and I know he'll give an unbiased opinion on what should be the course of action,' she explained.

'Good morning, Mr and Mrs Wetherby.' Connor gave them a charming smile and shook Dan's hand, then drew up a chair to sit in front of them. 'I believe you've been having some chest trouble. Dr Curtis tells me this has been worrying you for quite a while—am I right?'

His voice was kind and gentle, and the elderly couple, who had tensed noticeably as he'd come into the room, relaxed again. Victoria looked at him cynically. He could turn on the charm if he wanted to—his sympathetic manner showed a sensitivity she'd never experienced from him herself, she reflected.

Connor sat down in front of Dan, bending his head forward as he concentrated on the sounds coming through the stethoscope on the man's chest. After a minute or two he looked up at Victoria.

'Tachycardic and definite signs of consolidation at the left base,' he murmured to her. Then added, 'What was your advice?'

'I think Mr Wetherby needs to go to hospital for immediate tests, nebulisers and intravenous antibiotics.'

Connor nodded and stood up, folding his arms judiciously. 'I completely agree—no good pussyfooting around here.' He looked at the old man and his wife. 'Your chest is bad, and I can only see it getting worse, whatever we give you here. I think Dr Curtis has no alternative but to get you to St Hilda's immediately.' He added gently, to take the sting from his words, 'You'll feel so much better when you've had some treatment, believe me.'

Dan looked from one doctor to the other, then gave a sigh. 'Well, nowt for it, then. If you both think I should go, I'll have to do it. Mother, you'll have to get our Barry down from his place to give us a hand with the milking.'

'I'll do that,' promised his wife, 'when I've got you to the hospital.'

'I'm sending for an ambulance, Mrs Wetherby,' said Victoria. 'I want him to be started on oxygen as soon as possible, and the paramedics will give him that. Perhaps you'd like to follow him in your car.' She picked up the phone. 'I'll also speak to the registrar on the chest ward—we want things to get moving as soon as possible.'

Suddenly the Wetherbys looked very vulnerable and

bewildered—events had moved too quickly for them and they were in shock, gazing blankly at each other. Connor started to explain to them what was likely to happen in the hospital, his voice a low reassuring murmur. The phone calls over, Victoria looked at the trio for a minute. Connor was bending forward as he talked earnestly to them, encouraging them to ask any questions and giving them time to adjust to the situation. Quite an eye-opener, she thought. Connor had matured into the doctor with the perfect bedside manner!

'The ambulance is on its way,' she said. 'I'll go and meet them and fill in the paramedics on your condition, Mr Wetherby.'

In ten minutes the patient was on his way to St Hilda's. Susan started crying as he was taken out to the ambulance and turned to the two doctors waiting by her side.

'He's very ill, isn't he?' she said softly. 'I've known it for some time now—and I think he has, too—but we were both too frightened of the truth to do anything about it. How stupid we've been.'

'No, you haven't,' soothed Victoria. 'Lots of people find it hard to admit they need help. Look,' she added, 'let me give you a lift to the hospital—I don't think you should be driving after a shock like this.'

Susan shook her head and dried her eyes. 'No, no. I'll be all right. I'll go round by my son's place and he can come with me—he works from home so I know he'll be there.'

She got in the car and then wound down the window, looking up at Victoria and Connor. 'Thank you, you've both been very kind and I'm so grateful.' She smiled at them. 'You know it's like seeing a young Dr Sorensen and Dr Saunders when I look at the two of you—you're both so like your parents.

They were lovely doctors in the community, and it's so comforting to know that you're carrying on now they've retired.'

They watched as she drove out of the car park and Victoria murmured, 'A nice woman… She must have been so worried about her husband. It's amazing how some people have the capacity to carry on and ignore what's happening to them. He must have felt terrible for a long time.' She turned towards Connor and said with an effort at courtesy, 'Thanks for backing me up there—he's quite a stubborn old boy.'

'No question about it—he needs immediate treatment.'

They turned and went back towards the surgery, the autumn sun warm on their backs. Connor stopped for a moment and looked back at the valley in front of the house, the ploughed fields reflecting the shadows of the clouds as they drifted across the sky.

'It's a beautiful part of the world,' he said. 'I'd forgotten how lovely it was. My father was right about the surgery being in such an idyllic place.'

'Yes, and it all looks much the same as it did before I left some years ago. The stable block of Mum's house had just been converted into the medical centre then…' Almost absently Victoria added, 'Hard to believe such a lot has happened since.'

He looked at her with raised brows. 'Such as?'

She gave a short dismissive laugh. 'Oh, it's water under the bridge now.'

'Quite right, Freckles. Look forward.'

She frowned. 'I've told you, don't call me that.'

'Sorry…can't get out of the habit somehow.' He kicked a stone away from under his foot and glanced at her with a wry smile. 'Funny that we should end up together in this practice, isn't it? There was always a bit of rivalry between us in the old days—you probably never dreamt that our paths would cross again.'

'No,' agreed Victoria shortly. 'It certainly wasn't in my life plan.'

'We'll have to learn to work in harness together now.'

'I suppose so…'

'Perhaps,' he added thoughtfully, 'we could put on an act.'

'What do you mean, an act?'

He gave a short laugh. 'It's obvious, my dear Victoria, that you're not too keen about working with me.' He looked at her steadily. 'Perhaps you've good reason… I know I was a brat at school.'

Victoria was startled—he'd actually admitted he'd treated her badly! That was something, she supposed—a kind of apology.

'It was a long time ago,' she murmured.

'What I mean is that if we pretend that we rub along OK, we might actually find we do! After all, we could have quite a nice life here. We each have good homes to live in that our parents have vacated, even if it is short term—it just needs a bit of give and take on both sides, I reckon.'

His clear blue eyes held hers questioningly and Victoria suddenly felt rather flustered, as if a switch had been thrown to register a mixture of excitement and danger. She looked at him in confusion. For so long she'd thought of him with dislike, the memory of that dance assuming more importance than it warranted, she supposed. Now he'd acknowledged that incident, shown that he'd matured, and it seemed silly to hark back to how he'd treated her then. She looked at his strong, intelligent face and firm uncompromising lips and swallowed hard. How extraordinary was that? She was beginning to admit to herself that she found Connor Saunders just as sexy now as she had when she'd been a schoolgirl!

She stepped hastily away from him. She must be going mad or perhaps she was sex starved, but how could Connor Saunders, whom she'd vowed to put out of her mind, kick-start feelings she thought had vanished for ever? He looked at her enquiringly, obviously expecting some reaction to his remarks.

With an effort she collected her thoughts. 'I'm perfectly willing to work amicably with you, Connor, but it's got to be a two-way thing. For instance, your remarks this morning weren't very helpful.'

He held his hands up in submission. 'OK, so I'll try not to shoot my mouth off in future—and perhaps in return you can loosen up a bit.' Then he grinned and put his hand under her chin, lifting her face towards his as he inspected her face. 'How about it, Freckles? Think you can put on an act?'

She pulled her face away from his hand and said loftily, 'I shall act in a dignified way, Connor. We're both mature people—I'm sure we can manage to work together without bickering the whole time.'

'Hallelujah to that!' he remarked.

Karen, the practice nurse, ran towards them. 'Oh, Victoria, you wouldn't see one last patient this morning, would you? She's only about ten and has come in by herself—I don't think she's even registered with the practice, but she looks really poorly. Connor's still got another patient so he can't see her.'

Connor had started to walk back towards the surgery, his feet making a scrunching noise on the path. Victoria watched him go before she went with Karen to see the patient and sighed. Would Connor and she ever be able to get on normally with each other? Having to 'put on an act' might get rather wearing!

* * *

The young girl looked down at the floor, twisting her hands together.

'What's your name?' Victoria asked her gently.

'Evie Gelevska,' was the whispered reply after a long pause. 'I'm eighteen.'

'Can you tell me what's wrong, Evie?' Victoria probed, while doing a quick visual assessment of the young patient, a thin pale little figure dressed in a ragtag collection of old pullovers with holes in them and a skimpy skirt. There was an unkempt air about her, as if she hadn't bathed or washed for some time.

Evie looked up at Victoria timidly. 'My throat's sore. I thought you could give me something to make it better.'

There was just the hint of an accent in the girl's voice, a trace of a European inflection perhaps. She smiled kindly at her. 'I'm sure I can, Evie. Let me have a look at it. Open your mouth, pet, and I'll shine this torch on it to let me see better.' Victoria bent down and peered into her mouth. No wonder the poor girl was in pain: both tonsils were inflamed and there were white spots of pus on the periphery. She looked up at Evie's scared face.

'Poor you,' she said. 'It does look painful—but I can give you some medicine that will make it feel a lot better in a few days. Now I'll have to take some details about you first—you aren't registered with us, are you?'

She went round to her desk and opened up a new file on the computer for Evie Gelevska. 'What's your address?'

'I live at the bottom of Smithy Lane in one of the cottages there.'

Victoria nodded; she knew it well as the lane was behind her house. 'Right—and where's your mum? Couldn't she come with you?'

There was silence for a second, then the girl muttered, 'She's not well herself…but she's sort of used to it.'

Victoria looked puzzled. 'Has she got a sore throat, too?'

Evie hesitated, then said slowly, 'No—it's not that sort of illness. I mean she's OK really. Just finds it hard to get about.'

'I see. Have you just come to this area then?'

'Yes. We've only been here a little while.'

'Well, I do need your mum to come in because we'll have to ask her some questions about you and your general health—and she will need to register with us, too. Will you ask her to come when she feels up to it?'

Victoria printed off a prescription for antibiotics and handed it to Evie. 'Now, it's very important that you take this medicine properly—the instructions will be printed on the side by the chemist and you must finish them all. What school do you go to, Evie?'

'Braithwaite Comprehensive.'

'Well, I should take today and tomorrow off—after that, if you feel well enough, go back to school. And one more thing. I'd like to see you next week and just check that everything's all right. Make an appointment at Reception. Perhaps your mum would come with you next time—really it's better if I see her as well.'

The girl nodded, unsmiling. 'I'll come.'

'You know, if your mother's not well enough to come here, perhaps I could see her on a home visit…'

Evie's head jerked up and she said sharply, 'No! No, she wouldn't like that—I mean, she's not all that ill.'

Victoria frowned and looked gravely at Evie. 'She does know you've come to see me, doesn't she?'

A slight flush spread over Evie's cheeks, and there was a moment's hesitation before she spoke. 'Yes…yes, of course…

but she trusts me to do things myself.' Then she added abruptly, 'Thank you for seeing me,' and almost ran from the room.

Victoria followed her and then went into the office to look out of the window as she retrieved her bike and disappeared down the road. There was something odd about this situation, something that didn't add up, she thought uneasily. Why hadn't the mother rung the surgery to say that her daughter was coming in, especially as they weren't registered or known to the practice?

She started to pour herself a coffee from the percolator, then looked again through the window—she could just see Evie cycling down the hill to the village. Connor came into the room behind her.

'That coffee smells good,' he said, joining her at the window. 'What are you looking at?'

'Can you see that girl on the bike?' she asked. 'I feel worried about her… She came by herself and I'm sure the mother's unaware that she's been here.'

'What's the matter with her?'

'She's got a badly infected throat,' Victoria replied as she handed a cup of coffee to him, then added pensively, 'And she wasn't very forthcoming with information about her mother— didn't want me to contact her.'

'Why should she want to come secretly?'

Victoria shrugged. 'I've no idea—but I think I ought to pay the mother a visit—make sure things are OK.'

He nodded and sipped his coffee. 'Good idea. When in doubt, best to find out. By the way, don't forget we've a meeting at the pub tonight—about seven o'clock?'

'I haven't forgotten.' She sighed, her eyes following the vanishing figure of Evie Gelevska.

CHAPTER THREE

THE sunny weather of the morning had changed and now rain was lashing down. By the time Victoria had dashed across the road from where she'd parked her car to the Swinging Gate, she was soaked, her hair lying in bedraggled rats' tails against her collar. She stepped into the dark cosy bar of the pub and looked across the room, dabbing her neck dry with her scarf.

Connor was standing by the bar, talking to the landlord, but at that moment he turned round and saw her, surprised again when he looked across the room at the tall slender girl with the damp russet hair dripping onto her collar—nothing like the rather plump, bookish-looking schoolgirl he had known. The years had changed Victoria into a stunning, stylish woman.

He pushed his way through a knot of people and looked at her with concern. 'You look a bit wet… Go and get a table by the fire and dry out. What are you having, before we get started?'

'White wine, please.'

Victoria subsided into a chair and took off her coat, hanging it on the back of the chair. She watched as Connor made his way back with the drinks and sighed. He had a tough, no-nonsense look about him as he shouldered his large frame through the crowded bar, and she guessed he wouldn't give way if there were any contentious issues to be discussed that night. She pressed her lips together—she could be just as stubborn as he could if she wanted, but she did so hope they could get through the evening without bickering.

He sat down, passing a glass to Victoria and having a slow sip of wine from his. 'God, that feels good,' he remarked. 'I seem to have dealt with half the patients in the practice today. How was your first day?'

'Interesting, but I feel exhausted.'

'That's natural in a new job.'

It wasn't just the work, thought Victoria bleakly. The letter she'd received that morning had been hard to put out of her mind all day—her emotions felt as if they'd been through a shredder. She glanced at herself in dismay in the murky mirror on the wall opposite—her eyes had dark circles under them and her hair was wet through.

'Heaven's, what do I look like?' She sighed. 'I'm a complete wreck—I look as if I've just dived into a swimming pool.'

He looked at her damp hair clinging to her head as sleek as a seal's, and her glowing, flushed cheeks and said shortly after a second's perusal, 'You look OK to me. Have some wine—that'll make you feel better.'

'I could do with it,' Victoria admitted. 'It took me ages to do the visits, even with an *A - Z*. I haven't been back long.'

'Perhaps you could do with a satnav,' Connor suggested. He leant back in his chair and regarded her through narrowed eyes. 'You know, you've changed quite a bit since we were at school. I hardly recognised you.'

'Well, I don't have braces on my teeth or glasses now, but if it comes to that, you've changed physically as well,' she retorted.

His mouth twitched, eyes amused. 'What are you trying to say?'

'Just that…you've filled out, you're not so skinny. Still pretty opinionated, though,' she added boldly.

'I'd say you have a mind of your own, too. Your freckles are still there, of course—and your hair's the same auburn.' His gaze flickered over her and he took another sip from his glass. 'I suppose you got your tan in Australia. What happened to bring you back from there?'

Victoria said tersely, 'I got married, but it didn't work out. Enough said.'

He raised his brows slightly. 'Snap! I'm afraid my marriage has come to grief, too.' There was a flippancy in his tone, as if he thought the whole thing was of no account. No doubt he was a tough nut and someone who wouldn't give his heart easily, she thought. He probably thought of his collapsed marriage as a blip in his life, a setback rather than a disaster. If only she could be as detached as that, Victoria reflected. She wasn't really over Andy and perhaps never would be. She'd been desperately hurt over his betrayal, coupled with a cold anger that she had wasted five years of her life.

Her throat constricted suddenly. She'd tried not to think about Andy over the past few days, but today, of course, it had been impossible to block him out of her mind. For a second his handsome face danced in front of her and she was back in Australia, enjoying the thrill of surfing on the white rollers, laughing across at him as he crashed into the water with his board flying. They'd had such fun together, she thought, been so happy decorating their little house. And yet all the time she'd been completely blind as to what had been happening, stupid girl that she was… And now it was all over, and she had been left feeling destroyed, every confidence in her ability to attract a man shattered.

A sudden cackle of laughter in the pub brought her back to the present and she realised that Connor was looking at her with a quizzical expression.

'You were miles away, weren't you?' he observed.

'Sorry, just thought about something. I…I'm sorry about your marriage.'

He shrugged. 'Don't be—it was for the best. Carol and I had completely different outlooks on life.'

'So did my husband and I,' remarked Victoria.

'Then perhaps we have something in common after all,' observed Connor lightly, although perhaps there was something in his eyes that belied his flippant tone.

'I'm sure that the reasons for your splitting up and mine couldn't have been more different,' Victoria said stiffly. She wasn't about to open her heart about her past to a man like Connor Saunders. She got up and looked down at him. 'Another one before we get onto the subject of the practice?'

Connor's eyes followed her as she went to the bar, noticing how the men gazed at her in admiration. There were a few people in the room who remembered Victoria and came up to say hello and he noticed how the rather wistful expression on her face lit up in a warm sparkling smile when she greeted them. He could still hardly believe that the schoolgirl he'd called Freckles had turned into such a swan—she'd always had an attractive face, but the round National Health glasses and steel braces on her teeth had disguised her looks.

He remembered how he'd enjoyed competing with Victoria, but how stubborn she could be when they'd argued, always convinced that she was right! Oh, yes, sometimes she'd

seemed the most annoying and irritating female on the planet!
Had she changed her character as well as her looks? If she
hadn't, he thought glumly, then she'd be damned difficult to
work with.

He sighed to himself. It was going to be a terrific gam-
ble, the two of them working together—he hoped it wouldn't
be a hideous disaster. If there was one thing he'd learned
from the wreckage of his marriage it was that he would
never kowtow to a woman again. Years of having to placate
a spoilt and demanding wife had taught him the folly of
losing the upper hand, he thought grimly. No way would
he take a back seat in any working partnership, and he
would certainly make Victoria aware that he would do the
leading in the practice. She was probably a good enough
doctor, but when it came to decisions he would be the one
to make them.

'So what are you thinking now? You look very morose,'
Victoria said as she slipped back into her seat with the drinks.

'I'm thinking that the next stage of my life starts here—
and we've got to make the best of it.'

'That's right,' agreed Victoria. 'A bit daunting, isn't it?'

'Well,' he said briskly, 'let's make a start. What's first on
the agenda?'

'I think help for Maggie should be a priority. She really
shouldn't be doing all the filing, letters and reception virtually on her own. Lucy only comes in half-days and that's in
the afternoons.'

Connor nodded. 'I agree. If Maggie collapses, we're really
in the soup. Should we ask Lucy if she'll come in full time or
advertise for someone else?'

'Let's ask Maggie what she'd prefer. If she does want

someone else full time, we could still keep Lucy on as she is—there's enough work.'

They worked their way steadily through the issues that had been raised that morning, until Connor looked at his watch and grimaced.

'Let's give it a rest, shall we? It's been a long day and I think we've thrashed out a few things.' There was a sudden twinkle in his blue eyes. 'And do you realise we haven't come to blows either?'

'That's because I'm not an argumentative person—I'm easy to get on with,' she said pertly, actually forgetting under the influence of warmth and two glasses of wine that she disliked this man and didn't want to work with him.

He raised a sceptical eyebrow, then gave a sudden laugh, his face seeming younger, softer. 'Not argumentative, Victoria Curtis?' he said softly. 'Who are you kidding?'

'I'm *not* argumentative,' she began. Then she caught his eye and laughed. 'Not normally anyway…'

They stared at each other for a second. Something had happened between them that was rather incredible, thought Victoria. They were actually enjoying each other's company. And he was right—they hadn't disagreed once! It was almost embarrassing to find that they could get on, and that odd feeling of confusion began to send conflicting messages to her normally clear mind.

She looked hastily at her watch. 'It's getting late. I must get back and let the dog out.'

Amusement danced in Connor's eyes, as if he knew she was feeling flustered and perhaps rather enjoyed her embarrassment.

'You could stay and have something to eat, you know,' he suggested.

She shook her head, but before she could rise, someone got up from the chair behind and knocked against her. She turned round and saw with surprise that it was Janet Loxton, her first patient of that morning.

'We meet again.' Victoria smiled.

The woman gave her a brief smile. 'It's a bit crowded in here, isn't it?' she said, before walking out with the man she was with.

'You seem to know quite a few people here,' remarked Connor.

'She was my first patient today. Practically demanded sleeping pills from me. She seemed to think I should just give her what my mother had prescribed without any questions. Maggie filled me in on her background—her father's quite a celebrity round here apparently. He's Bernard Lamont...'

'The painter?' said Connor with interest. 'There's a whole gallery devoted to his work in Glasgow. Do you know it?'

Victoria shook her head. 'Afraid not—I'd be interested to see some. I do know he's very old and driving her nuts because she says he's very demanding.'

'Sounds a familiar story, I'm afraid—'

His voice cut off as a sudden tremendous noise from outside rocked the whole room with the reverberation. There was a collective scream from the people inside, then all the talking and laughter stopped abruptly and shocked faces turned towards the exit where the sound had come from. Connor and Victoria's eyes met in consternation as peripheral noises of breaking glass and screams from outside gradually petered out into an unnerving silence.

'What the hell...?' Connor stood up, pushing the table away from him. 'Sounds like there's been an almighty crash. We'd better go and see what's happened.'

He strode quickly towards the door, saying briskly to those in the way, 'Excuse me, we're doctors. Could you let us through please?'

Victoria felt the familiar surge of adrenalin she'd felt when she was working in A and E and there'd been a red-light RTA. She forgot her tiredness, her longing to go home to a hot bath and bed, and followed Connor to the door, psyching herself up for whatever horror she was going to witness.

Outside the rain was still lashing down, the droplets lit by the lamps in the square. Just in front of the pub two cars had crashed into the railings by the pavement and were embedded into each other. One or two other cars had been hit by the crashed vehicles as they'd spun across the road—Victoria could clearly see that one of the cars was hers, its side stoved in and crushed against a lamppost.

'Oh, God... This doesn't look good, Connor,' she said grimly.

'Absolute carnage,' he muttered.

A figure lay on the ground close to the cars and incongruously the thump of heavy metal music was still coming from one of the vehicles, as well as the blare of a horn that was jammed.

Connor turned back to the pub landlord, who was following him. 'Jack, get emergency services while we look at the victims,' he yelled. 'Tell them it's a multiple RTA with at least two or three casualties—and bring us some torches from the pub.'

Both doctors ran to the scene where some people were bending over the injured figure and another man was looking into the cars. A young girl was standing by the victim, crying and trembling with shock.

'Help my mum. Please...do something for her,' she hic-cupped through her sobs.

One of the onlookers said, 'I think we ought to move this poor woman inside—she's going to get pneumonia.'

Connor pushed through them. 'Don't move her!' he shouted. 'She might have injured her back or neck. Can we get through to see her, please? We're doctors.'

'There's a young lad in that other car,' said the man, pointing to a crushed vehicle a few yards away. 'His door's jammed and his legs seem to be caught under the steering-wheel... you'll need someone strong to get him out. There's a strong smell of petrol about as well.'

'I'd better take him, then, and perhaps you'd help me open the door,' said Connor to the man. He turned to Victoria and said in a low voice, 'Do you feel able to take on this lady? She looks pretty bad.'

Victoria felt a stab of irritation—must he make it so obvious that he doubted her ability, and how dare he diminish her authority?

'I guess my training and experience were every bit as good as yours—I did spend five years in A and E in Australia after all,' she snapped sarcastically. 'You get on with the young boy—I'll concentrate on this patient.'

She turned to the frightened young girl staring at her stricken mother on the ground and said briskly, trying to instil some normality and authority into the situation, 'We'll do our best for your mum. Keep calm and perhaps one of these good people can lend you a coat to put around you.'

She dropped to her knees beside the injured victim and began examining her, as Connor splashed his way through the puddles, accompanied by the man, and went to the passenger side of the car in which the youth was trapped. He and the man used all their strength to wrench the door open, and having grunted and heaved for a minute or two it eventually creaked open. He shouted to try and make himself heard above the pounding music from its radio and the blasting car horn.

'Hello! I'm a doctor—I was just in the pub opposite. Are you hurt?'

A youth with a baseball cap on turned frightened eyes to him. 'My legs are stuck—I can't move them. And the bloody wheel went into my stomach.'

He did look very young, suspiciously young to be driving a car, thought Connor. He crawled into the passenger seat and peered down at the youth's legs. The impact seemed to have thrown the seat forward, pushing the youth's legs under the buckled steering-wheel. Connor reached across the boy's trapped body and turned off the ignition key. There was blessed silence as the music and the horn were turned off simultaneously. Vaguely Connor noticed that his own cheek had scraped against something sharp as he'd bent forward to turn the key off, and that the blood that was dripping onto the car seat was his. He ignored it and spoke loudly and clearly to the youth lying back in the seat, white with shock.

'It's better without that radio and horn on—I can hear what you're saying now. What's your name?' he asked.

'Brett Canfield,' he muttered.

'Well, can you wiggle your toes, Brett?'

He nodded. 'Yeah.'

'And can you feel the pressure on your legs?'

Brett grimaced and blinked as if pushing back tears. 'Yeah—it hurts.'

'At least you've got sensation there,' said Connor reassuringly. 'Now, don't worry, help's coming in a few minutes. Just try and breathe slowly. I'm sure they'll get you out soon—I don't want to injure you further by pulling you out without someone to help me.'

'Are the police coming?' There was panic in the young man's eyes. 'If you can get me out, I can get home by myself.'

Connor frowned. 'Sorry. No way can you get home by yourself—you'll have to go to hospital for assessment. And as for the police, of course they'll be coming as they do to all traffic accidents.'

'Do me a favour, will you?' Brett looked pleadingly at him. 'Can you give me that coat on the back seat and put it round my shoulders?'

'You cold?'

'Er...a bit. But I don't want to leave the coat behind, that's all.'

Connor pulled the coat forward and draped it round the boy, then turned back as he heard the sound of an ambulance, its siren whining down to silence as it arrived, together with a police car. Two paramedics jumped out and ran towards him, their fluorescent green coats gleaming in the dark.

'Right,' said one of them, squatting down besides the driver's door. 'What's the story?'

'I'm a GP and that's my colleague,' explained Connor tersely. 'We were in the pub when the accident happened. This is Brett Canfield—his legs are trapped but still have sensation and he may have internal injuries from the steering-wheel. His pulse is fairly rapid but I feel that we ought to move him from this vehicle as quickly as possible—there's a strong smell of petrol around.'

'OK,' said the paramedic briskly. 'Before we try and move you, Brett, we'll take your blood pressure and put a collar round your neck—you've possibly got whiplash.' He turned to Connor. 'I see he's not wearing a seat belt.'

'Don't believe in them,' muttered Brett thickly.

'Perhaps you'll try using them next time,' commented Connor, as the paramedic wound a cuff round the boy's arm preparatory to taking his blood pressure. By this time another ambulance had arrived and was dealing with the victim still lying on the road. A police officer came towards the car and squatted down next to the paramedic dealing with Brett.

'How is he?' he asked.

'We don't know until he's been X-rayed. Hopefully not too bad. I dare say you can interview him at the hospital fairly soon.'

The policeman nodded and started to inspect the vehicles, taking a note of their numbers, their positions in the road and the damage done to them. The jammed driver's door was forced open, and as Brett was gently lifted out onto a stretcher his jacket slipped from his shoulders onto the road.

'Put my jacket back round me,' he said urgently. 'I need it.'

'Keep calm, lad—we've got blankets here we'll put round you. Much more satisfactory.'

'No!' shouted Brett, struggling to sit up but pressed back by the paramedic. 'I want you to put it round me!'

'We'll put it in the ambulance next to you—we won't lose it.'

The paramedic gave it to his colleague and a small package fell out of one of the pockets. The man bent down to pick it up, then looked at it carefully.

'What do you think this is?' he said quietly to Connor.

Connor looked at the transparent little packet carefully with his torch. 'Can't be sure, but it could be cocaine or something similar.'

'That's what I think—I'll hand it over to the boys in blue.' The man gave a weary grimace. 'This lad's probably been driving under the influence of drugs—they'll certainly do some blood tests when we get to the hospital.' He looked closely at Connor's face. 'You look as if you've gashed your cheek, mate. Let me clean it up for you.'

'No, no, I'll look at it later,' said Connor impatiently. 'I must see if I can help Victoria now—you get going with Brett.'

The man shook his head. 'You should get that seen to soon.' Then he banged the doors to on the back of the ambulance and climbed in the front. It started to move off, the tyres swishing through the puddles and spraying Connor's trousers liberally with water. He looked across at the huddle of figures bent over the prone figure of the woman, their silhouettes illuminated by the streetlamp above them. Victoria was gesturing to him, her voice urgent.

'Connor—over here! Quick, I need you!'

'What's happened?' he asked as he ran across to join them.

'This lady's in trouble,' said Victoria crisply. 'She's losing blood like a sieve from somewhere, BP's 70 over 40 and she can't breathe. I'm sure she's got a traumatic pneumothorax—she probably fractured a rib during the impact and punctured her lung. I'll have to put a tap in her chest before she's moved—she won't last if we wait till she gets to the hospital.'

'What can I do?' asked Connor, noting with approval Victoria's efficient way of handling the situation and her cool assessment of the woman's condition.

'The paramedic's got a bag full of tricks there—let's get some dextran into her and replace some of the fluid she's losing. Will you put in a line?'

The woman's daughter was making little noises of fright and terror. 'Will she be all right? What are you doing to her?' she cried.

'It's all right,' said Connor, his voice steady, trying to communicate reassurance to the young girl as he started to set up a drip. 'We're going to get this liquid into her—it's a chemical compound that can be used as a substitute for blood in an emergency.' He glanced up at the girl. 'What's your name?'

'Zoe…Zoe Jennings. My mum's called Brenda.'

'Well, Zoe, why don't you go with Jack, the landlord, and have a nice cup of tea inside while we help your mum? I know she'd not want you to get wet.'

Jack took the frightened child inside, and Victoria felt the woman's abdomen. She looked up at Connor. 'Definitely a pneumothorax. There should be some lignocaine there in that bag. Give her a shot and if Bill swabs her chest and puts some towels around the area, I'll put in a drain.' She frowned, trying to assess the woman's condition, then said tersely, 'Get that Haemaccel in more quickly if you can.'

Connor nodded, wryly appreciating the crisp way she gave instructions, and squeezed the bag gently to increase the rate of flow.

The rain was still beating down and two of the policemen were holding a tarpaulin over the victim and the medics to protect them. The pub landlord reappeared with a large lamp, which he trained on the scene. A few yards away a small crowd of onlookers was gazing in fascinated horror at the dramatic tableau.

'Pass me a scalpel,' directed Victoria as she pulled on some surgical gloves. 'Keep an eye on her BP, Bill. Connor, hold that bag firm while I make an incision—we've got to get this blood out of the chest cavity or it will put tremendous strain on her heart.'

Victoria traced the line she needed to cut with her left

index finger, then she made a one-inch incision into the chest wall, while Bill, the paramedic, swabbed away the blood. Connor watched her absorbed face as she concentrated on the job, her hand steady and firm, oblivious to her surroundings. He felt a sudden twinge of embarrassment that he'd implied earlier that she couldn't handle the situation. She was good— very good—calm as a cucumber, her hands deft as she prepared to put the drain into the woman's chest and get rid of the blood that was preventing the woman's lungs from expanding when she tried to breathe in.

The tube Connor handed her had one end in a transparent bag, and she pushed the other end firmly into the incision. Bill handed her a needle and suture and Victoria anchored the drain in place with a stitch between the skin and tube.

'Keep your fingers crossed,' she muttered.

There was a tense silence for a few seconds, then with a hiss the trapped air in the woman's chest cavity escaped through the tube and into the collecting bag.

Victoria closed her eyes for a second. 'Whew!' she muttered in relief.

'That's helping her BP—it's coming up nicely,' said Bill, squinting at the dial on the Dynamap that was monitoring the victim's blood pressure. 'It's 100 over 65 now.'

'Her colour's improving,' noted Connor, his fingers holding the woman's wrist as he felt her pulse. 'Pulse is getting stronger.'

Victoria sat back on her heels, puffing out her cheeks and running her fingers through her hair. 'Then you can take her off to hospital now—at least she's stabilised.'

She got up and watched as the woman was gently lifted into the ambulance. Even by the poor light of the streetlamp

Connor could see Victoria's face was grey with exhaustion and the strain of the past few minutes.

'That was brilliant, Victoria,' he said quietly to her, squeezing her shoulder. 'You saved her life—no doubt.'

She looked up at him, a grin creasing her tired face. 'I'll admit now that it's a long time since I did that procedure.'

'Good job you were here,' said Bill. 'Thanks a lot, Doc. Be seeing you!'

The ambulance drove off, its siren whining eerily in the darkness, leaving the two of them standing in the rain together. The people watching drifted back to the pub and just a few policemen were left at the scene with the pub landlord, Jack Fordham. He came forward and patted Connor and Victoria on their backs.

'Great stuff, both of you! Will you come in and have some soup and a bite to eat—on the house of course? We'll see to the young girl, get in touch with her relatives.'

'That's kind of you, Jack, and thanks for the offer, but I think we'll get back to our homes and dry out.' Connor felt in his pockets and pulled out his car keys. 'Come on, Victoria, I'll give you a lift. Looks like your car is one of the cars that lad hit—we'll have to get it towed away, I guess.'

Victoria sank back exhausted into the passenger seat of Connor's car, her head spinning in reaction after the tension of the last half-hour.

'Well, the first day at the practice has been a baptism of fire,' she remarked wearily.

Connor eased the car carefully through the debris on the road. 'I reckon you've patched up a pneumothorax a few times before—you did a very good job.'

Victoria gave a short laugh. 'I'm glad I didn't have too

much time to think about it.' She flicked a sardonic glance in his direction. 'You were rather concerned that I wasn't up to it, weren't you?'

A wry smile crossed Connor's face. 'My apologies... I needn't have been worried at all. Talk about cool, calm and collected...'

A small smile of triumph crossed Victoria's face. Perhaps he was beginning to realise he wasn't so very superior to her!

She turned to look at his strong profile and softened slightly. 'I don't think that young paramedic had ever seen a pneumothorax before and it was reassuring to have you there— someone who knew what they were doing,' she conceded.

Connor's mouth twitched slightly in amusement at her restrained compliment as they waited at the red lights on the main road. 'We made rather a good team, don't you think?'

A funny thing, Victoria reflected. An hour ago she wouldn't have ever imagined that Connor and she would do anything in harmony!

'What about the lad in the car?' she asked.

'He'll be OK, although he's probably got whiplash. The paramedic found what looked like drugs in his pocket—I think he'll be questioned about that.'

In a few minutes they had arrived at The Cedars and as he parked the car, Victoria switched on the car's internal light and noticed the gash on Connor's cheek, still oozing blood.

'You need a Steri-Strip on that,' she observed. 'It's quite a deep cut. I've got some in the house that I can put over the wound.'

'I'll be all right—don't fuss.'

She clicked her tongue in exasperation. 'I thought we

weren't going to argue. You don't want the damn thing to get infected. For God's sake, come inside and we'll have a cup of tea while I dress it.'

She let them into the warmth of the house and Buttons the dog gave her a frantic welcome.

'Hello, Buttons, darling—I'll give you your supper in a moment,' she said, patting the Labrador on the head and then putting on the kettle.

As she opened a cupboard where she kept some Steri-Strips her eye caught the envelope with the letter in it that had arrived that morning. She'd thrown it on the worktop in distress when she'd read it, but the events of the past two hours had put it out of her mind. Suddenly its contents came flooding back, but now wasn't the time to reread it. She threw some tea into the pot and poured boiling water over it to let it brew while she dressed Connor's cut.

'Stand still under the light while I clean it up a bit,' she said, looking critically at the jagged cut.

Connor sighed. 'If you must. I don't think it's necessary, though.'

'I said stand still,' said Victoria tersely.

He shrugged and stood obediently while she swabbed the wound with a piece of cotton wool dipped in dilute disinfectant. Her face was very near his, so close that she could see the evening stubble on his chin and dark flecks in his blue eyes. She could smell the male smell of him, almost feel the solidity of his presence next to hers.

It had been a long time since she'd stood so intimately near a man, and on this day of all days, and with shocking unexpectedness, she felt a longing for someone to hold her body close, to feel a man's face next to hers. She still felt shaky after the tension of the evening and less able to cope with the shock of the letter she'd received. Rarely had she felt so vulnerable and lonely. For a second she closed her eyes, almost imagining herself in Connor's embrace. Then she opened them in embarrassment and hurriedly finished sticking on the tape.

'All finished,' she said briskly, stepping back to survey her work critically. 'And a pretty neat job if I may say so…' She turned away, washing her hands at the sink, hoping her expression hadn't revealed her thoughts. 'Would you like a cup of tea?' Then she added quickly, 'Or perhaps you'd rather get home?' Better to get him out of the house before she had any more mental aberrations.

'Very nicely done,' he commented, squinting at her handiwork in the mirror. 'And, yes, tea would be nice.' He looked at her critically. 'You're absolutely soaking—why don't you go and change while I pour out the tea? No good getting pneumonia on the first day of work!'

She was wet and cold, but she hesitated. 'I can wait…'

'Victoria,' he urged in exasperation, 'for God's sake, don't argue. You've had your way with me,' he said with a grin. Then he added gently, 'Now, do as I say. Go and change. Buttons and I can keep each other company for a few minutes. We've had a busy evening and you look exhausted.'

And suddenly, perhaps because of the reaction after the tension of the accident, perhaps because of Connor's concern for her, but mostly because of the letter and its contents, tears began to pour down her face. She turned away, acutely embarrassed, and scrabbled for a handkerchief.

Connor frowned and pulled her round to face him. 'What the hell…? Victoria, what is it? Tell me. Has something happened?'

'I…I'm sorry, Connor, I don't know what's come over

me,' she snuffled, blowing her nose and blinking back her tears. 'It's not been a good day, I'm afraid. Take no notice.'

'Is it what I said to you—about our school days? If so, well, I apologise. I didn't mean to be rude.'

She shook her head, almost impatiently, and half laughed through her tears. 'Oh, no, Connor—after all, I was used to you teasing me at school!' She looked down, twisting her hands together, then said bleakly in a small voice, 'The thing is...well, this morning I had a letter informing me that my divorce has come through. I knew it would come some time, but it was still a shock.' Then she added slowly, 'Funny, that— with a thing as simple as a sentence on a page my marriage has ended. I'm single again!'

Connor looked down at her silently for a second, his startling blue eyes filled with concern, and he tightened his hold on her arms slightly. And it seemed at that moment almost natural for Victoria to rest her head on his shoulder and allow herself to relax against him as his arms went round her waist and drew her towards him. She could feel the comforting thump of his heart against hers, the solidity of his broad frame, and for a second she was aware of a funny sensation of being protected, safe from the shock of a broken marriage and the years she'd wasted.

He put his head down to hers and brushed her forehead with his lips.

'Poor old Freckles!' he murmured. 'I know only too well how you feel—but you'll get over it in time.'

His eyes were very close to hers—she could see green flecks in them and the little creases of laughter lines at their corners. She closed her eyes for an instant, imagining for a daft moment that he was going to kiss her and that she would feel his cheek rough against hers. Then almost in a trance she blindly pulled his face to hers, offering her lips to his, pressing them to his firm mouth, as if by doing so she could obliterate the memory of Andy and his betrayal from her mind. Her arms went round his neck and she leaned her body into his, and somewhere within her there was a lick of treacherous response to a man she didn't know, didn't even like.

Then a little warning voice in her head whispered, This is wrong, don't be such a fool. She felt Connor's hands on her shoulders, gently pushing her away. Opening her eyes, she was aware of him looking down at her in a puzzled way, and she leapt back in acute embarrassment, her face scarlet. What the hell had she been thinking of—what had made her come onto him like that? A moment of madness had put her in the most embarrassing situation, with Connor of all people…

'I...I'm sorry. I didn't mean to tell anyone. It just came over me all at once that I really was no longer married to Andy,' she almost gabbled.

He nodded and said lightly, 'It can be a blessing to finally cut the ties of an unhappy marriage, you know. It's not all bad news. Look on the bright side—you're your own person again, not beholden to anyone.' He smiled at her. 'Now, go and change those wet clothes.'

Connor probably thought she'd had a brainstorm—no wonder he'd tried to put the brakes on her mad behaviour. She must have seemed so predatory—she'd lost one man so seduce another one as quickly as possible! She felt hot with shame and fury at herself.

Why on earth had she confided in him, of all people? She'd wanted him to believe that she was tough, could cope with anything life had to offer. That image had been shattered a moment ago, she thought wryly, when she'd revealed so much of her inner self and her vulnerability to a man like Connor.

The most unbelievable thing of all, of course, was that she'd loved it—the hot feel of his lips on hers, the comfort of his hard body against hers, and that prickly feeling of doing something dangerously exciting. Her heart pounded with a mixture of disgust at herself and a thrilling kind of energy.

'I'll go and put some dry things on, then,' she muttered, and almost ran upstairs. Whatever she'd felt when kissing Connor, however, she doubted that he was right in his assertion that she would get over her broken marriage. The thing was, she couldn't imagine any man taking Andy's place. Neither could she trust her judgement to have any kind of relationship with a man again.

Connor slumped down in a chair and absent-mindedly stroked Buttons's ears as the dog leaned against him. Funny how things could turn round in a few seconds—Victoria Curtis was a stunning-looking girl, but until now he'd thought of her merely in terms of a fellow pupil with whom he'd been at sixth form college. Since his bitter break up with Carol, he hadn't thought much about girls or sex—oh, no, after that experience he was going to steer a very clear path away from women! The last thing he wanted was any entanglement with the opposite sex—once they got their claws into you your life was not your own. That was why he was so shaken at the response he'd felt when Victoria had pressed herself against him, her soft lips so warm and sensuous against his. He'd thought he was immune from all that stuff…now he'd better be on his guard, and it would be a long time before he'd succumb to another female.

Connor sighed heavily as he remembered his life with

Carol—trapped in a relationship with someone who'd been driven by a selfish regard for her own needs. She was a beautiful woman whom he'd loved passionately at first, would have done anything for when they first got married. He'd been blinded by that attraction, he thought bitterly—it hadn't taken long to realise that greed and boredom fuelled her life and that she would never be satisfied with what he had to offer her. Sex did not equate with love and commitment any more for him—he'd learned his lesson.

CHAPTER FOUR

'YOU'RE not serious? You say the car's a complete write-off?' Victoria grimaced at the phone in her hands as if it was to blame for the bad news, and Maggie, who was standing beside her in the office, looked at her enquiringly.

'Well, have you got a car I can use for the time being until I can sort out another one?' Victoria made another face at Maggie, indicating that the person on the other end of the line couldn't help her there either, then put the phone down with a sigh.

'No luck?' said Maggie sympathetically. 'That's the trouble with a small country garage—they've no stock. It sounds as if you didn't have a very good evening.'

'It wasn't the best,' admitted Victoria, a sudden chill going through her as a replay of the scenario of the evening before flickered through her mind. She swallowed and tried to sound upbeat.

'The miracle was that no one was killed—luckily Connor and I were on the spot.' She pulled a telephone directory from the shelf and started to leaf through it. 'I'll just have to hire a car, I suppose—but I'll need it today. I hadn't realised mine had been totally wrecked in the accident outside the pub last night.'

Oh, God. Again a vision of what had happened at the end of the evening seemed to dance in front of her eyes. Victoria bit her lip. What a hideous embarrassment that had turned out to be! The fact that her car had been written off seemed a mere irritation compared to what had followed, with her practically forcing Connor Saunders, of all people, to kiss her.

She'd thought that the formality of ending her marriage would almost have come as a relief—but when the letter had arrived, the finality of it, the waste of all those years when she'd thought Andy and she had been so happy, had suddenly hit her very hard. She'd made a fool of herself and Connor probably thought she was going after him because her marriage had ended and she needed a man—any man!

He'd merely been trying to comfort her but, like a sex-starved idiot, she'd reacted with a passion that had taken her by surprise. Even now she could recall herself not only responding to the sensation of his body close to hers but encouraging him to go on. If he hadn't gently pushed her away… She shuddered for a second, thinking that it could have led to anything, the state she had been in.

'Life goes on, Victoria,' he'd said drily as he'd left. 'It's tough, but you'll just have to keep going and forget about your life in Australia. As my father said, you're damn lucky that you've got a job in a beautiful part of the world here. Count your blessings.'

His manner had been quite brusque, suddenly changing from the concerned tone he'd had before she'd thrown herself at him. Perhaps he had been trying to show her that if she had sudden designs on him, it was a futile exercise. As if, she thought scornfully to herself. From now on she'd have to make quite sure he got the message that what she'd done had been a momentary aberration, and that he was the last man on earth she'd go for.

'I'd lend you my car,' said Maggie, breaking into her thoughts, 'but it's gone for its MOT.'

The phone rang and Maggie turned away to answer it as Connor and Pete came into the room, engaged in earnest conversation.

'Ah—glad we've caught you, Victoria,' said Pete. He handed her a letter. 'The health authority has sent us this jolly missive—I wanted you both to comment on it. Connor's already read it.'

'And a damn silly idea it is,' growled Connor. 'Absolutely typical. Nothing's been thought through. They want to dump a breast-screening unit in our tiny car park.'

Victoria took a deep breath as she flicked a look up at Connor—she had to appear relaxed and professional as if nothing had occurred between them the night before. The scar on his face gave him a rather piratical look. She ran her eyes down the page.

'They do say that if we don't allow it there won't be any breast screening for the next year in this area…that's blackmail, but we can't let the women here down.'

'And tell me where the hell the patients and, more importantly, ourselves are going to park—down that busy road? Or do they expect us to forget our cars and do our calls on foot?' said Connor sarcastically.

'Exactly,' said Pete. 'That's a very good point.'

'Just a minute,' interrupted Victoria, frowning. 'We need to discuss this further. It's absolutely essential that this area is covered for breast screening.'

'So you'd just allow the health authority to park their socking great screening unit in front of the surgery, blocking out any space should we need an ambulance or if disabled people need close access? They're just holding a gun to our heads with talk of no breast screening if we don't agree to it. There must be other places.'

Connor looked mulishly at her and Victoria almost smiled as she saw a glimpse of the schoolboy with attitude on his face. He'd always liked his own way and that hadn't changed very much, it seemed. He had a point, but she wasn't going to give in until they'd discussed the whole thing properly.

'Yes…OK. It's going to be awkward—but how many women are we going to put at risk if we veto it? For goodness' sake, it's only for a few weeks. I think we ought to talk to them about it before we dismiss it out of hand,' she said with spirit.

'Give the health authority an inch and they'll take a mile,' grunted Connor, then he shrugged. 'However, if you have the patience to talk to them, go ahead.'

Victoria frowned. She imagined it was typical of Connor to blow his top without dreaming of mediation in this sort of situation. And yet she'd seen another side of Connor yesterday besides the impatience he sometimes exhibited. She recalled how kind and reassuring he'd been to the Wetherbys when Dan had been taken to hospital and his reassuring back-up at the scene of the accident the previous evening. He was a complicated mixture, she decided.

'I'll say that we'd like to discuss it with them face to face, then,' said Pete tactfully, stepping in as he poured himself a cup of coffee. 'I believe you had a busy evening,' he added to Victoria, adroitly changing the subject. 'I'm sorry to hear you've no car now. What are you going to do for transport?'

'I'll hire a car, but it won't come till tomorrow.'

'I can cover for you,' said Connor. His eyes flickered over her face. 'You OK after last night?' His tone was fairly neutral—he could have been referring to the accident or the way she'd come onto him the night before.

'Absolutely fine,' she replied coolly, flicking a hair carelessly from her face. She was going to show Connor that any emotion—and other things—she'd displayed last night had been a temporary glitch, and now she was completely in control. 'And, yes, that would be great if you could help me out today by doing my home visits.'

She turned briskly to go to her room, but Maggie called out to her as she was leaving.

'Victoria, just a minute. I've just had a call from Janet Loxton. You remember she was your first patient yesterday? She says she wants you to come urgently—she sounded very upset.'

'Won't I do?' asked Connor.

'She did insist she wanted Victoria, but to tell you the truth it was all rather garbled—a bit hysterical. Something to do with her father.'

'That's funny. Yesterday she really tried to put me off making a home visit, and now she's asking me to go and see him,' said Victoria, frowning. 'Her father's ninety-six so anything that's happened to him could be serious.'

'Then I'll take you,' offered Connor. 'I'm visiting St Hilda's to find out what it has to offer and more about the plans to close it. It might be a good idea for you to see it as well—we could go after you've seen this patient.'

Victoria felt slightly wrongfooted—did she really want to be alone with Connor so soon after last night's embarrassment? Surely he wouldn't want to be too close to her either?

'Er…perhaps I could borrow Pete's car?' she said in desperation.

Pete shook his head. 'Really sorry, but I've got to go to a

health authority meeting in Leeds, and I'm a bit late now as it is. I'll probably try and get this problem of the screening unit put on the agenda.'

It seemed there was no help for it. Victoria sighed and picked up her medical bag. 'We'd better go, then,' she said rather grimly to Connor, thinking how awkward the next hour or so was going to be.

Connor backed the car out of the parking space and Victoria sat bolt upright in her seat, gazing steadfastly out of the window.

'Better put your seat belt on,' suggested Connor. He turned to look at her before they drove off. 'So you're feeling better today?'

'I told you,' said Victoria shortly. 'I'm fine—absolutely fine. I…I'm sorry I got a bit…er, over-emotional last night. It was just rather a shock to realise that I was finally divorced, that's all, and reaction after that accident.'

'Of course it was,' agreed Connor smoothly.

Victoria flicked a covert look at him. There was a slight smile on his lips. Damn him—probably revelling in her embarrassment. They drove in silence to the end of the village where Janet and her father lived in a neat Victorian semi, the kind of house that estate agents would say was 'desirable' both in its position and design. Connor parked the car in front of the door.

'So this is where the great man lives—very nice,' he remarked. 'Like me to come up?'

Victoria shook her head. 'If I need you, I'll let you know,' she replied briskly.

She leapt out of the car and Connor watched her as she ran up the steps and rang the bell. His thoughts drifted to the events of last night, and how out of the blue Victoria had kissed him—had actually pulled him towards her and pressed her lips to his. He could still feel their soft fullness, their sweet taste in his mouth, feel the imprint of her body against his. Of course he knew she hadn't meant anything by it—that she'd done it because she'd been upset and distraught about the end of her marriage—but it had had an unsettling effect on him.

Victoria was a complicated mixture, he reflected—quick to flare up and voice her own opinions, but she'd been efficiency itself last night at the accident. He ran a distracted hand through his rumpled hair. He had to admit he couldn't take his mind off the way her body had felt against his, and how difficult it had been to wrench himself away from her. The extraordinary thing was that he was very well aware that Victoria had been just as turned on as he had been. He gripped the steering-wheel in his hands, unconsciously setting his face in a determined scowl. He would never allow himself to take that emotional road again. A sexy woman had brought him great unhappiness before, and he wasn't about to do a rerun of that.

He stared straight ahead of him down the street, unaware of the traffic going by. He'd been living a bachelor life for some time now since Carol had left him, and he had to admit the sensation of an attractive woman flinging herself at him was new and tantalising. Carol had been a high-maintenance woman, and he wouldn't say they'd ever been happy together—especially towards the end when she had betrayed him so cruelly, but he had tried to keep things going in the belief that marriage was for life. And now? For the first time in many months he had begun to feel a sense of liberation, an optimism about the future. And he wasn't about to compromise that with Victoria Curtis.

* * *

Janet opened the door to Victoria looking very different from the immaculate woman who had seen Victoria yesterday at the surgery. Her hair was unbrushed, her face devoid of make-up and her eyes red with crying.

'You've got to help me,' she croaked. 'It's my father—I can't get him to wake up. He's upstairs in his bedroom.'

She turned and almost galloped up the stairs and Victoria followed, wondering at the change in her. Janet stopped before she went in and turned to Victoria, twisting her hands together in agitation.

'He's always awake by now. I...I think I've done something to him. It's all my fault. Perhaps he's...' Her voice trailed off and she began to sob uncontrollably.

Victoria put her hand on the woman's arm. 'Let's see what's happened,' she said gently.

Janet's father lay on the bed in the spacious room, which was filled with paintings on the walls and heavy furniture. Two large armchairs were on either side of the window, which was framed with heavy curtains in a rich red brocade, and near the door was an easel with a large painting on it. Victoria had the brief impression of stepping back into a different era, a slower world.

She went up to the bed and put her finger on the old man's carotid artery in his neck—there was a steady slow pulse.

'He's still alive, Mrs Loxton,' she said, then she raised his eyelid and noted the slow reaction to light in the pupils and frowned. 'Is he on any kind of medication?'

There was a silence, then Janet shook her head. 'No...er, that is, he won't take anything—except for his two tots of whisky at night.'

'It looks almost as if he's been drugged...' began Victoria.

Then she stopped and looked at Janet with a sudden flash of insight. An old man who was a nuisance, who stopped his daughter from having a social life, and a lonely woman who'd formed a new relationship—a woman who'd demanded sleeping pills…

'You said you thought you'd done something to your father,' she probed, looking at Janet's blotchy face. 'What did you mean?'

Janet looked away from Victoria's gaze and bit her lip. 'I don't know what I meant—at least, I was only trying to help him. He gets very agitated.' Her lips trembled and she dabbed at her eyes with a handkerchief.

'Come on, Mrs Loxton—Janet—you must tell me what's happened. Have you given something to him to knock him out? Sleeping pills perhaps?'

The woman gave a little gasp, and stammered, 'How…how did you know? It was only one or two, and it was just to give me a little peace when I went out last night, otherwise he wouldn't have let me go.'

Victoria began to pat the old man's face gently. 'Get some black coffee, a damp cloth and a bowl with water in it,' she said tersely. 'We'll try and rouse him. I expect the whisky didn't mix well with the triazolone. And while you're downstairs, ask Dr Saunders to come up—he's waiting for me in the car.'

A minute later Connor entered the room and Victoria gestured to him. 'I can't lift Mr Lamont alone—can you help me get him propped up a bit?'

'What's happened to him?' asked Connor as he pulled the old man up onto his pillows.

'His daughter gave him some of her sleeping pills to keep

him quiet,' replied Victoria tersely. 'It didn't go well with the whisky he has at night.'

'Good God—was she trying to kill him?' Connor looked across at Victoria in amazement.

'Not at all. I think she only wanted some space for herself.' Victoria bent forward to the old man's ear. 'Wake up, Mr Lamont. Open your eyes, please… I'll see how his reflexes are.'

She took a pencil and ran it under the patient's foot, giving a nod of satisfaction when the foot curled in response to the stimulus. Janet came in with a mug of coffee and a bowl with a flannel in it.

'Is…is he all right?' she said tearfully.

'Hopefully when we get him to wake up he won't be too bad.' Victoria began to sponge the patient's face and neck with the cool water and he stirred a little. 'Hold his head back, Connor. I'll try and get some coffee into him.'

Mr Lamont's eyes fluttered and he obligingly opened his mouth slightly. His daughter sprang to the side of the bed and grasped his hand.

'Oh, Father, thank God. I thought I'd… Well, I didn't think you'd make it. Oh, thank the Lord!' She buried her head in her hands and started to sob silently.

'What are all these bloody people doing in the room?' Bernard's voice was slurred and he looked at Victoria and Connor in bewilderment. 'Janet, what's happening?'

Janet looked speechlessly at the two doctors as if unable to think of anything to explain their presence.

'You've been rather unwell,' said Victoria quickly. 'Your daughter was worried when you seemed to be sleeping very deeply, so she did the right thing and called us—we're doctors.'

He scowled at her. 'Well, I'm all right now—so you can go, can't you?'

'Not before I take your blood pressure,' said Victoria firmly. Ignoring his furious look, she wound the cuff of her sphygmomanometer round his arm and inflated it.

'I don't give you permission to do this,' growled Mr Lamont.

Victoria grinned at him. 'I'm a little deaf, Mr Lamont— I'll listen properly when I've finished.' She watched the dial on the machine and smiled. 'Not too bad at all. Now, what was it you wanted to say?'

To her amazement a slight smile appeared on his old face and he looked at her wickedly from under bushy eyebrows. 'By God, girl, my eyesight's pretty poor, but I can just about make out what you look like, and I'm surprised my blood pressure isn't sky high, with you taking it…'

Victoria snapped her medical bag shut and laughed. 'You really do seem a lot more awake now, Mr Lamont. What about some lunch? I don't want you to get up until you've had something to eat.'

'You're a bully,' he grumbled. Then he frowned at them. 'What happened to make me feel as if I've emptied the whisky bottle, then? Two glasses doesn't normally give me a hangover.'

'It's probably something that will never happen again,' Victoria assured him. She stood up. 'I'll come back and see you in a few days just to make sure you're OK.'

'You don't need to—I can't stand bloody fuss.'

'I'm sorry, Mr Lamont. I seem to have gone deaf again,' said Victoria pertly as she walked across the floor to the door. There was a gleam of respect in the look that the old man gave as his eyes followed her out of the room.

Downstairs Janet stood like a naughty schoolgirl before them, her head down, nervously twisting her hands together.

'What are you going to do?' she whispered to Victoria. 'I didn't mean to harm him—truly, truly I didn't. It's just that my life has been completely taken over by him. If anyone asks me to do anything or go anywhere, I can't do it. And he's such a tyrant. Now he can't paint he feels life isn't worth anything.'

'Mrs Loxton—Janet—look, I know it's not easy looking after a cantankerous old man, but the fact of the matter is that you should never, ever give anyone medicine that has been prescribed for you. You know you could have killed him, because although the triazolone I prescribed is low dosage, given enough and mixed with the whisky it could be fatal.'

'I know, I know,' wept Janet. 'I only wanted an hour or two away from him—just make him snooze a little. I didn't realise that it would be so serious. You do believe me, don't you?' Then she added in a sad little voice, 'I do love him very much, you know.'

'Yes, I believe you,' said Victoria gently. 'But I can't just leave it there, Janet. If you've reached the stage when you start reacting like this, we must at the very least bring in Social Services...'

'He won't let me.'

'He will. I'll explain that he's got to give you more time to yourself, that you must have a rest.' Victoria turned to Connor. 'We're going to the community hospital in a minute, aren't we? Why don't we see if it's possible to get respite care for Mr Lamont for a week or two?'

Connor nodded. 'It's worth a try, I suppose.' There was a coldness in his voice that surprised her.

She turned back to Janet. 'We'll be off now. Ring us if you're worried about him and make sure he has something light to eat. And don't give him any more triazolone! I'll ring you later today and tell you whether we've managed to get a place for your father—and I think Social Services will be coming round later as well.'

In the car Connor switched on the ignition and started to ease out into the traffic. 'You're happy with that decision, are you?' he said quietly.

Victoria looked at him sharply. 'Of course. Why shouldn't I be?'

'Frankly, I think you've let that woman off very lightly. Surely you should let the police know in this sort of scenario?'

'Oh, come on. She was at her wit's end. She's been looking after him for years. When you're at the end of your tether, you do desperate things.'

'Things that might have led to the man's death,' said Connor grimly. 'No matter what strain you've been under, you can't do that sort of thing. There are people to call on… Social Services…'

'He wouldn't let her. She did try and get people in to help but he sent them packing.'

'So you don't think she's done anything against the law?'

Victoria flushed angrily. 'I think to involve the police would be taking a sledgehammer to crack a nut. Janet Loxton isn't a bad woman—she loves her father very much. She was just driven up the wall and couldn't cope.'

'If you say so…'

'I do say so,' snapped Victoria. 'I'm convinced she didn't want to harm her father. She was stupid and ignorant, but she isn't cruel. I think she's learnt her lesson and I think if anything good has come out of it, it's meant something has to be done to help her.'

Connor frowned, his blue eyes looking sharply at her. 'God, you're stubborn! You don't know her well enough to assume all that. If she ends up murdering him, what will you feel then?'

'Don't be ridiculous. Janet Loxton admitted to giving him sleeping pills and she's had a terrible fright. Anyway,' added Victoria angrily, 'she and her father are my patients, and I will take responsibility for them. And I'm not being stubborn.'

They had reached the hospital and Connor drew into a parking space and stopped. They glared mutinously at each other, and then a sudden memory of what had happened the night before when they had been alone together seemed to hit them at the same time, and each dropped their gaze. They stepped hastily out of the car, banging the doors impatiently behind them and walking in eloquent silence up to the entrance.

How dared Connor interfere in the management of her patients? fumed Victoria, sliding a hostile glance at him as she stomped up the hospital steps. She might have known he'd be like this: shades of his attitude to her at school—doing it just to wind her up, to show that he knew best and maintain some sort of spurious authority over her. She heaved a sigh of frustration. It was Sod's Law that she should be working with one of the most awkward men she'd ever met, however good he was at coping with an RTA or comforting someone who'd just learned she was finally divorced...

St Hilda's Community Hospital was in an old Victorian building in the middle of Braithwaite, built of the yellow brick the Victorians had favoured and boasting a large clock tower which the townspeople used as a landmark to meet friends. Outside were large banners posted on the wall with 'Save St Hilda's for the people of Braithwaite' written on them and invitations to come to various fundraising events.

Victoria looked up at it before they went in. It was a familiar building she remembered from her childhood, and on occasion she had visited friends who had been patients there. Now its uses had been expanded to include a minor injuries unit in a small casualty department and one of the wings was devoted to the rehabilitation of people who needed help after major operations or strokes. Connor had an appointment to see the medical director, who had a cramped office at the side of the small courtyard in the centre of the building.

He strode over to the office and Victoria almost had to run to keep up with him. He was obviously going to talk to her as little as possible—Connor hadn't liked losing the argument about Janet.

Brian Ingleby invited them to sit down, removing a tottering pile of papers from the chairs and replacing them on the window-sill. He had a harassed air and looked as if he'd got dressed in a tremendous hurry with a tie pushed askew under his collar. He'd taken his jacket off and rolled up his shirt-sleeves, which gave the impression of someone deeply immersed in his work.

'Good to see you,' he said. 'I've been wanting to meet The Cedars' new GPs—we really need your support to keep this place going.'

Connor extended his hand. 'We're looking forward to learning a bit more about the place.' He turned to Victoria and said coolly, 'By the way, this is Victoria Curtis, née Sorensen. You'll know her mother, no doubt.'

'Of course, of course, just as I know John, your father,' said Brian, smiling at her and seemingly unaware of any under-currents between her and Connor. 'It was quite a surprise when Betty and John got married, but marvellous news. They were great supporters of ours.'

'The hospital's certainly in a great situation to provide a community service,' commented Victoria. 'It seems to offer so many facilities—the minor injuries unit, for one thing, wasn't here before I went away.'

Brian nodded. 'Everyone finds that incredibly useful and, of course, it takes the pressure off the main casualty unit at Sethton. We've also got a respite wing to give carers a break.'

'I was going to ask you about that,' said Victoria swiftly, flicking Connor a quick hostile glance. 'I've got a patient whose daughter could really do with some help. He's not an easy old man, and I'm sure his first reaction would be that he doesn't want to come in at all—but is there any hope of a bed for a few days?'

'I'll take you over to that department,' promised Brian. 'In fact, I want to show you everything, because when I've done that I'm absolutely sure that you'll be as passionate as I am about saving this place from the supermarket they want to build here instead of keeping what is an absolute gem of a place.'

And it was a gem of a place, thought Victoria when they'd been taken around and had seen the various departments and wards. As Connor put it, 'St Hilda's offers the personal contact and intimate setting that is often missing in huge hospitals—and, of course, it's so convenient for the local people.'

'So I'm sure you'd like to join our fundraising committee,' said Brian with a grin. 'We really need two people like you to organise the sponsored run we're having to raise money for the appeal—are you on for that? It would be easy for you to meet to do the finer details, seeing you work together.'

Connor and Victoria looked at each other frostily, but with Brian Ingleby gazing at them with such enthusiastic good humour it was obviously hard to refuse.

'Er…well, I'm sure we'd be pleased to do anything to help,' Connor said rather weakly.

Brian slapped him on the back. 'Great! I know the local practices are keen to back us up—one or two are having dances, car boot sales and so on, and so I'm sure we'll be raising a good deal of money.' He turned to Victoria. 'What about the respite care unit—did you talk to the social worker about your patient?'

'Yes, I'm glad to say that there is a bed available, so I'm going to go and tell Mr Lamont and his daughter that he can go there for a little while. I'm sure it will help both of them.'

'Good, good. I think your patient will be very happy when he comes here—it seems to make all the difference to stressed families to have someone else take over for a while. Some of them are often near breaking point and it gives them a much-needed break. And I bet Mr Lamont will be keen to come again when he knows what it's like.'

'I'm sure you're right. And thank you so much for showing us around.'

As they walked back to the car Victoria couldn't resist giving a tiny smile of satisfaction. She looked pertly up at Connor. 'Brian seems to think these respite care units do a lot of good.'

'I'm sure they do.'

'But you still think I'm doing the wrong thing?' she persisted.

Connor stopped for a moment by the car before unlocking it, and looked at her over the car roof. 'As you said, they're your patients.' Then he added unexpectedly, 'But if it works then perhaps it is for the best. I'm prepared to go along with what Brian says.'

But not prepared to go along with what I think, thought Victoria crossly as she settled herself into the car and glanced at his profile under her lashes. 'I didn't know that you ever admitted you could be wrong, Connor,' she said caustically.

He grinned as he shoved the car into gear and edged into the road. 'I'm usually right—but very occasionally I can be persuaded there could be another point of view.'

Victoria sank back into her seat and laughed softly. 'Now, that's an admission I never thought I'd hear,' she murmured.

'Just don't count on me changing my mind very often, that's all.'

'I won't,' she promised grimly.

CHAPTER FIVE

THE email was brief and to the point. 'John and I are having a brilliant time in South Africa, touring the Drakensberg Mountains—the weather, food and scenery are wonderful. We are well and loving the rest, although looking forward to seeing you in a few weeks on our return. We do hope that you're both finding life at The Cedars enjoyable and settling down easily to work with each other, love Betty and John.'

Victoria stared in irritation at the screen and wondered what to reply. 'Glad you're having a good time. I am going slowly mad with Connor, he loves winding me up all the time…'?

Hardly the right thing to send to her mother and new stepfather in the idyll of a delightful honeymoon. The thing was that she would enjoy work very much more if she didn't have to combat Connor's verbal spats every day. Then she wound her hair thoughtfully round her finger as she reluctantly admitted to herself that if Connor wasn't there, perhaps work would lose some of the edge and stimulus she was almost beginning to relish.

She frowned at the email again—there were other considerations besides her exchanges with Connor. Her mother's reference to the happy couple's homecoming meant that perhaps it was time for her to start looking around for her a place of her own—she certainly didn't want to be a lodger in the place where her mother and John were going to live. Of course they might want to live in John's flat, where Connor was living now—it would be good to know what their intentions were going to be.

Victoria looked up from the computer screen. She could see Connor through the open door to Reception. He was leaning against the counter, his long legs crossed, talking to Maggie and laughing, which made his face look younger and softer than it normally did. In fact, he looked like a doctor who might appear on a TV soap—rugged good looks combined with an impressive physique, and when he was in a good mood a great sense of humour. She bit her lip. Why was it that her thoughts strayed so often to the wretched man, although he was so annoying? In contrast, her thoughts of Andy seemed to have receded so that he had become a sad memory of what might have been.

Averting her eyes hastily as Connor came into the room, Victoria looked with renewed diligence at the screen.

'There's an email from our parents here,' she said. 'They're both well and seem to be having a good time.'

'Lucky them,' commented Connor.

'They hope we're enjoying working together,' she added drily.

Connor's eyes met hers, one brow raised. 'And are we?' he asked. He came over to the desk and looked down at her with amusement in those piercing blue eyes that she felt deciphered every thought she had in her head. 'Well?' he demanded.

She shrugged. 'It depends what mood you're in…'

He grimaced and squatted down beside her, holding her

glance in his. 'What you mean is, when I agree with you, everything in the garden is fine—but if I dare to express an opinion then working with me is impossible?'

Victoria swallowed. Ever since that first evening at work when she'd almost seduced him, she'd tried to avoid being too near Connor, although sometimes she thought wistfully that she wouldn't mind having a rerun of that assault on her senses! Now he was so close to her she could see his ragged hairline: his thick fair hair had been rather badly cut and stood up in a little quiff over his forehead. Her eyes flickered to his mouth and an image of it being firmly clamped to hers whipped through her mind. Then she pulled her gaze away quickly, trying to ignore the absurd way her heart had begun to thump against her ribs.

'Perhaps we'll get used to each other,' she said a little breathlessly.

He looked at her thoughtfully for a second. Her cheeks were slightly flushed, long lashes forming a curve on her cheeks when she looked down, glossy hair pinned back to reveal her slender neck.

'Let's hope so,' he remarked, suddenly gentle in tone. Then he stood up abruptly and went over to the filing cabinet and started rummaging through some papers. 'Do you know where Maggie keeps the blood results?' he asked, his voice a little rough. 'I can't find the damn things.'

'They're on the desk,' said Maggie, coming into the room. 'By the way, I had a word with Lucy and she'll be delighted to work in reception full time now her youngest is at school— she's getting her sister to pick the little boy up.'

'That's great,' said Victoria. 'That will help you, and us, a lot.' She stood up from the desk and stretched, suddenly relieved that Maggie had come in and broken an awkward moment between her and Connor. 'I'd better go and do one of my visits before lunch—and then, heigh-ho, an afternoon off!'

'We need to talk about this sponsored run for St Hilda's before the weather gets too cold and it starts getting dark early,' said Connor, looking up from the sheaf of papers he was leafing through. 'I hope you'll be entering, Maggie—and all the others, of course.'

Maggie laughed. 'I don't think I could run round this building, let alone round a proper course.'

'Do everyone good to get in training for it…' He hesitated for a second then said to Victoria rather diffidently, 'I was wondering if we could use the land at the back of your house that goes down to those woods? What do you think?'

'I don't see why not. We could get a very good circuit if we used the field and the woods at the bottom.'

'Then perhaps we could go round it soon.' He glanced out of the window. 'It's a lovely day—what about after you've done your visit, in the lunch-hour? Have you got to go far out to see the patient?'

Victoria put her jacket on and picked up her bag. 'Actually, Evie Gelevska, the girl I'm seeing, lives at the bottom of the lane that goes round the back of our garden, so I may as well walk.'

Connor looked at his watch. 'I've nothing much on until a diabetic clinic later this afternoon. If I came with you now, we could kill two birds with one stone.'

The flutter of excitement she felt at the prospect of being alone in the countryside with Conner alarmed Victoria for a second, then she gave herself a mental shake. Why on earth should it bother her that a colleague should want to discuss the sponsored

run with her and look over the course? The man wasn't propos-
ing a mad affair with her—just a walk down the field!

They started off down the lane at the side of the field—it was
a perfect autumn day, the air with a fresh bite to it, a blue sky
and a crackling carpet of fallen leaves on the ground. Victoria
had collected Buttons from the house and he was bounding
enthusiastically ahead of them, stopping every now and then
to examine a rabbit hole or tearing off suddenly on a futile
mission to catch a squirrel.

Connor had taken off his tie and stuffed it in the pocket of
his anorak so that his shirt was open. He looked relaxed and
casual and incredibly sexy, thought Victoria, hastily remind-
ing herself that this was just an objective assessment.

'Buttons—come back here, boy!' she shouted, more to
distract herself than really wanting to call the dog back.

They came to a cattle grid across the lane and on the other
side there was an enormous muddy puddle. Buttons took a
stylish leap across the grid and landed joyfully in the water,
covering himself liberally in mud. Victoria stopped and
looked doubtfully at the situation.

'Are you going to copy Buttons?' asked Connor, looking
in amusement at her dilemma.

'I'll manage…'

'I'll lift you across,' offered Connor. 'My shoes don't matter.'

'Please, Connor,' said Victoria firmly, 'I'd rather you didn't.
Really, I'm perfectly capable…'

She teetered over the grid and then with an almighty effort
tried to propel herself over the puddle, but just failed to clear
it, landing with an ungainly splash and covering her black skirt
with muddy water. Connor's hands went out and caught her

arms before she actually sat down, hauling her out beside him. He looked down at her with dancing eyes.

'I've said it before and I'll say it again—you're one stubborn girl, Victoria. If you'd let me help you as I suggested…'

'I'm absolutely fine, thank you. Everything can go in the machine,' said Victoria shortly, watching Buttons, who with a sharp bark rushed off to tackle another squirrel.

Connor dropped his hands from her arms. 'Suit yourself. I just didn't want you to fall,' he remarked. He bent down and flung a stick towards Buttons, watching in amusement as the dog pranced up to it and began carrying it proudly around in his mouth. Then, seeing a squirrel again, Buttons dropped the stick and resumed the chase.

'Has he ever caught a squirrel?' Connor asked. 'And does he ever stop?'

Victoria brushed her skirt with her hand and laughed. 'I don't think so—but he never gives up. I must say it's so convenient having the surgery next to the house, because every lunchtime I can take Buttons out—it does us both good. By the way,' she added, 'the email from my mother mentioned that they'll be home in a few weeks. I think I'm going to start looking for my own house and move before they come back. I need a place of my own. Will you stay in your father's flat?'

'It's only small, and I certainly don't intend to stay there.' He frowned pensively. 'You ought to come round some time because there's a lot of old stuff from the practice there that you might like to see before it's chucked out. I'm sure my father won't want to live there with Betty. By the way, why are we going to visit Evie Gelevska at home?'

'I want to find out why she never came back for her follow-up appointment. I saw her struggling through the village with a huge bag of shopping last week—she certainly wasn't attending school.'

'Was she the girl who came on our first workday without her mother?' asked Connor.

'Yes. I just feel slightly uneasy about Evie's health and her mother's. She was so cagey about her mother not coming with her.'

The cottage was one of two quite a distance down the rutted lane—a long way for a young girl to carry a lot of shopping, thought Victoria. They were standing at the top of a slope and all around them was the glorious view of rolling moorland beyond the woods and the bright sun throwing dramatic shadows across the ploughed fields.

Victoria took a great gulp of air. 'It's so good to be in this part of the world,' she murmured. 'It's like breathing champagne…'

'So you don't miss Australia? No regrets about leaving it?'

She was silent for a moment then shrugged. 'If I—that is, Andy and I—had had children then I might have had regrets. Luckily we didn't, so the worry of bringing them up in their birth country or moving them here a long way from their father when we split up didn't arise.'

'You say "luckily". Did you not want a family?' enquired Connor lightly.

She sighed and looked up at a buzzard wheeling above them. 'I always said there was plenty of time for that sort of responsibility—something to look forward to in the future. Frankly, I was having so much fun without children I never gave much thought to it.' Then she grinned at him. 'Anyway, I've got Buttons now—animals are less hard work than children, don't you think?'

Connor nodded. 'I imagine so…'

There was something indefinable in his voice that made Victoria look at him curiously. 'You and your wife never had children either?' she ventured.

He turned away from her for a moment and gazed at the view over the woods to the moors, his hands clenched in his trouser pockets, and gave a short laugh. 'Kids? No…no, I haven't any children.'

'So that was quite lucky in a way—I mean, with you being divorced,' she said quickly, thinking that he sounded as if children were low on his scale of priorities.

Connor's expression was unfathomable. 'Lucky indeed,' he said drily. 'After all, children are a full-time commitment.'

He sounded less than enthusiastic about having a family and Victoria wondered if part of the reason for his split with his wife had been because she had wanted children and he hadn't been interested.

'Did your wife work?'

'Oh, yes. Carol's a high flier. She's an editor on a woman's magazine, and very much in demand as a speaker and a journalist.'

The slightly bitter note in his tone hardly registered because he turned quickly to her and indicated that she should go before him on the path down to the woods, flicking a look at his watch and changing the subject.

They approached the property, looking at it for a minute before Connor observed, 'The best thing about this place is the view of the dales in front of it—it looks as if it's practically falling down.'

Victoria nodded, noting that the small garden was a tangle of long grass and nettles and looked very neglected. The front door was slightly open and the sound of a radio playing music floated out to them. She knocked loudly on the peeling green paint of the door.

'Hello! Anyone at home?'

The music stopped abruptly and the clip of shoes walking on a stone floor came towards the door. It was opened fully and Evie's pale little face peered round with wide scared eyes at the two visitors. Then she obviously recognised Victoria.

'What have you come for?' she asked abruptly. 'I'm all right now—I don't need to see a doctor.' She frowned, and looked with hostility at Connor. 'Who is this man?'

'He's the other doctor at the surgery—Dr Saunders. We're just taking my dog for a walk and I wanted to make sure you were all right. You never came back for your follow-up appointment, did you?'

'I'm better. I didn't need to come back.'

Somewhere in the background a young child began crying and Evie looked behind her nervously. A little boy, a toddler, emerged from a back room, weaving an unsteady gait towards them. He stopped and looked at them with big eyes like Evie's.

'Darius, go back to Mummy,' said Evie, bending down to him. The child remained immobile, sucking his thumb.

Victoria said gently, 'Could I come in for a minute? I'd like to speak to your mother if I could…'

Evie looked confused, a little frightened. 'She's busy. She doesn't want to see people anyway.'

'I only want to—'

A voice called out from the back. 'Who is it, Evie? What do they want?'

Victoria's eyes met Evie's. 'Go and ask her if she'd see me, Evie. I'm not here to intrude at all, just to see if you're both all right.'

'Wait here, then. I'll have to see if it's OK.'

Evie ran off into the back regions, leaving Victoria and Connor on the doorstep, with Darius, a stout little figure bundled up in thick hand-knitted clothes, still staring at them, occasionally giving a hacking cough.

Victoria looked around the room. The place was bare of furnishings with a plain stone floor and a wooden table with some books on it in the corner—rather bleak but clean. She heard the sound of voices, then the figure of a woman came slowly and painfully from the back, leaning on a walking stick. She looked like Evie, with a narrow sallow face and dark hair scraped back into ponytail.

'You must be Mrs Gelevska, Evie's mother.' Victoria smiled. 'I came just to make sure she was all right…'

The woman's expression was sullen, and she said in a heavily accented voice, 'You didn't have to come. Evie's fine. In fact, I don't know why she came to see you.'

'You didn't know that she'd come to the surgery? It was a good thing she did—her throat was badly infected.'

'She should have told me first,' muttered Mrs Gelevska.

'Yes, it would have been good if you could have come with her,' said Victoria gently. 'However, I see from your walking that it would be difficult for you to get to the centre without transport. It's a long way down the lane to the main road.'

There was a short pause, then Mrs Gelevska said reluctantly, 'Do you want to come in for a moment then?'

Victoria stepped into the room where Evie stood by a small fire burning in the grate. There was an odd air of tension in the room as both mother and daughter stared at her watchfully, as if expecting her to say something untoward.

'You look much better now, Evie,' said Victoria. 'I saw you in the village the other day—do you do all the shopping?'

'Sometimes…' The girl glanced at her mother, as if wondering that she'd said the right thing. 'We don't need much, though.'

Victoria turned to Mrs Gelevska and looked down at the woman's hands still holding her walking stick. Some of her fingers were misshapen and puffy. 'I see you've got rheumatoid arthritis—are you on medication? It must be very painful.'

'I can cope.' The mother had a closed expression on her face that didn't encourage further questions.

'I could give you something that would relieve the symptoms,' Victoria persisted. 'If you let me do a blood test, we could find out exactly what type of arthritis you have.'

Evie looked up at her mother. 'Please, Mum, let the doctor do something to help you. You're in such pain and I felt so much better when I'd been to see her.'

The woman hesitated, then said, 'Will I have to register with you?'

'Is that a problem?'

The mother and daughter looked at each other, then Mrs Gelevska whispered, 'I don't like the authorities to know about me. I'm not sure if I have permission to stay here…'

'If you come from most places in Europe, it shouldn't be a problem,' remarked Victoria, opening her medical bag and taking out a prescription pad. 'What is your country?'

'Poland. We came over two years ago, but my husband…died.' Mrs Gelevska wiped her eyes. 'He was such a good man, but I feel so ignorant about all the laws here.'

'I'm so sorry,' said Victoria, looking at them with compassion. 'It must be desperately hard for you both. Do you have anyone to help you do the shopping and washing besides Evie?'

The woman sank down on a chair and covered her face with her hands. 'I knew it! I knew it! You're asking these questions because you're going to take my children away from me, aren't you? You think I can't look after them too well, and you'll tell the social people and they'll come for them! Is that why this man is with you—has he come to spy on us?'

'Not at all,' said Victoria in astonishment. 'He's my colleague and we certainly haven't come to do that. I truly just came to see if Evie was better.'

Mrs Gelevska started crying. 'I will send the children back to my sister rather than send them into care—but I will miss them so much.'

Victoria met Connor's eyes, who gave a brief shake of his head. She went over to Evie's mother and put a hand on her shoulder. 'Please, don't think about that. We can get help for you. I know it's beautiful out here but it's very isolated. I'm sure the council could get you something nearer the village.'

'The council will say I'm too ill to look after Evie and Darius.'

'They won't do that—but they might offer you help that would give Evie a rest. And you know that the child shouldn't have to do as much as she does and go to school.'

'I know, I know,' said Mrs Gelevska bleakly. 'She does too many things for me.' She looked searchingly at Victoria. 'Are you sure that my children won't be taken?'

'You must allow me to speak to the social workers because they can draw up a plan to help you.'

Little Darius had a sudden paroxysm of coughing and Connor sat down on one of the chairs and took the child gently onto his knee.

'That sounds nasty,' he remarked, stroking the little boy's head and smiling at him. 'Perhaps you've caught what your sister's had—we'll have to give you some magic medicine to make it better.'

Darius's lip wobbled and Connor felt in his pocket and brought out a little wooden bear with movable arms. 'Here you are,' he said. 'This is Charlie. He's got a cough, too. Will you look after him for me?'

A smile spread across Darius's chubby face, and he examined Charlie carefully before stuffing him in his cardigan pocket. 'My bear,' he said cheerfully.

Connor looked up at Mrs Gelevska and Evie with a grin. 'I always have a bear or two in my pocket for our little patients— they're better than doctors for making a child feel better!'

He smiled as he watched the small boy toddle happily away, belying Victoria's assumption that he wasn't interested in children. From the tender way he'd dealt with Darius it was plain that they held a significant place in his heart. Funny that he should have given her the impression that he and his wife hadn't wanted a family.

She shrugged to herself—it was none of her business anyway. She turned to Mrs Gelevska and started to scribble out a prescription.

'Look, I'll take these to the pharmacist in Braithwaite—one for you and one for Darius. The pharmacist will deliver them back here—no need for Evie to get them. And I'll be back in a day or two with someone to discuss everything you might need.'

The woman and the girl looked at her silently and Victoria smiled at them. 'Please, don't worry…and I'll see you both very soon.'

'Thank you…thank you, Doctors,' whispered Mrs Gelevska as Victoria and Connor let themselves out.

'Poor thing—she's obviously been absolutely scared stiff

that her children would be taken into care. I guess Evie's been doing all the shopping and cleaning—and missing school in the process,' said Victoria as they made their way down the path to the field, with Buttons bounding ahead. 'Mrs Gelevska seems very isolated and unsure of her rights. I'll have a word with the social workers to try and sort out better accommodation nearer the village.'

'I hope they won't be too heavy-handed—it's quite a delicate situation,' remarked Connor.

Victoria bit her lip and nodded. 'I know, but I've got to help them somehow. They can't go on as they have been.' She flicked an appreciative look at him. 'Your touch worked like magic with little Darius,' she remarked.

'I can't bear to think of that mother even contemplating sending him back to Poland,' he replied tersely. 'Children should be with their mothers—and fathers—if possible.'

'Your mother died when you were very young, didn't she?' said Victoria gently.

He nodded. 'My father did his best, but it was difficult for him. For many years I spent the school holidays with my aunt and her husband—not a happy arrangement.' His laugh was slightly bitter. 'They disliked children—found them a nuisance. I wasn't made to feel welcome.'

'That's very sad,' said Victoria, a sudden glimmer of sympathy and understanding for the life the schoolboy Connor had endured. He'd had to learn to stand on his own feet, and perhaps that was why he was so aggressive sometimes.

Connor shrugged and said briskly, 'All water under the bridge now.' He looked down at her with a grin. 'Look, we can't take on the worries of the Gelevskas now. Let's enjoy the day and sort out the course for this run.'

He was right, Victoria acknowledged. It was better to step back from problems sometimes and not get too closely involved in her patients' lives. They reached the dry stone wall at the edge of the field and Connor opened the gate where they stood for a moment, enjoying the view of the river beyond the woods winding in a silver ribbon towards the rolling moors. Above them the buzzard was still quartering the skies, and everything seemed very peaceful.

Connor looked at his watch and started striding down to the river. 'Now, let's see how long it would take to do the circuit. As I remember from years ago, it goes round Daniel's Leap—the waterfall at the bend in the river. I estimate it could take forty minutes if it's decent weather—most people could manage that.'

'I'd forgotten about the waterfall—do you think that could be dangerous? The path can get very slippery,' panted Victoria as she tried to keep up with Connor.

'It's had very good fencing put up in the last few years, but we'll have a good look at it…'

Buttons had disappeared, plunging joyfully into the woods, and after a few minutes they heard him barking furiously.

'I think he's found something else to chase,' remarked Connor. 'This place is a paradise for him.'

They were in the wood now, and the sound of the waterfall was getting louder. They turned the corner, catching their breath at the sight of the tremendous cascade, swollen by rain, plunging several metres down into the pool below, before the river rushed on over huge boulders. Connor pointed to the new fencing that surrounded the steep sides.

'That looks safe enough,' he shouted above the noise. 'Poor old Daniel—he never had a chance,' he added.

'Who was Daniel and what happened to him?'

'Don't you know the story?' asked Connor, smiling down at her. 'Legend has it that Daniel was escaping from his father, who was trying to stop him reaching his love, Miranda. He was meant to marry someone else. Miranda was waiting for him at the other side of the waterfall. It was in full spate as it is today. He tried to leap over and missed his footing and died in the attempt. That's why it's called Daniel's Leap.'

'That's terrible…' Victoria stared down at the tumbling depths of water and shuddered. 'I hope it's not true.'

'Can you imagine leaping over that to get to your true love?' teased Connor. 'Or would you let him go?'

'I don't know. Perhaps I'd look for a bridge…'

He laughed. 'That's very practical—but not romantic. You wouldn't take a chance for love?' His blue eyes held hers questioningly for a moment and she blushed.

'I've already taken a chance on love—and lost.' She shrugged, leaning against a tree for a moment as she watched the cascade pouring over the rocks and the froth of the spray flying up. 'I'm never going to take that chance again.'

Connor nodded. He agreed with that sentiment himself, didn't he? Then he thought wryly how negative it was—just because one dish disagreed with you, were you never to eat again?

'I suppose we shouldn't give up on life because of one mistake,' he said thoughtfully, putting a hand out to brush back the hair that had whipped over her face. 'That would be a tragedy.'

His eyes ranged slowly over her slender figure relaxed against the trunk of the tree, an unreadable expression on his face. She was still breathless from the brisk walk they'd had up to the waterfall, her hair tousled, cheeks slightly flushed, and she felt his glance skim across the rise and fall of her breasts before it came to rest on her face. And suddenly she felt once more the dangerous butterfly flutter inside her of desire, and there was something exciting and exhilarating about being alone with him—and in this setting something dangerously intimate. A flicker of electricity rippled through the hairs of her neck and she knew that something was going to happen in the heightened atmosphere of Daniel's Leap.

Perhaps he also felt that the mood between them had changed, for he stepped back from her and was quiet for a second, as if trying to defuse the charged atmosphere.

Then he folded his arms and said gently, 'Tell me, Victoria, just what was it that your husband…er, Andy, did to hurt you? Don't tell me you both "grew apart" from each other—that old cliché—or that he fell for another woman.' Connor's voice was soft, his gaze on her intense. 'I can't believe that any man would abandon you. What on earth was it that broke up your marriage?'

Victoria sighed. The reason for Andy's leaving had left her devastated. It was something she wanted to put out of her mind, fearful that if she dwelt on it she would never recover the confidence she needed to get on with her life. She had given everything to her marriage, believing it to be rock solid. How wrong could she have been? She bit her lip and looked at Connor's strong face. He seemed to have found it easy to get over his broken marriage, and perhaps he would laugh at her if she told him the reason she and Andy had parted.

She had never wanted to talk about it—it was over and done with, wasn't it? And, of course, it showed what a deluded fool she'd been. But in this place, with the dark wood surrounding them and the roaring waterfall as a backdrop, it felt suddenly right to unburden herself a little of the hurt she'd been carrying. After all—why keep it a secret now?

'The thing is…' she started haltingly, and Connor came nearer to catch her words over the thundering water as her voice dropped. Then she slowly gathered pace, as if the dam that had been holding her words back had burst. 'The thing is, Connor, Andy didn't fall for another woman—that might have been easier to cope with.' She gave a short bitter laugh. 'The fact is, he fell for a man—a man who'd been to our house many times. Andy was gay, and for all the years I was with him I never realised it. And so, you see, I was in love with an illusion, in love with a person that didn't actually exist.'

CHAPTER SIX

THE sound of the waterfall thundering down the rocks was like the finale of some dramatic symphony as she finished speaking, and she watched Connor silently, wondering how he'd react to her revelation. He looked stunned for a second, his eyes wide with shock.

'You poor thing,' he murmured. 'That was bad news.'

Victoria continued sadly, 'We had such fun, Andy and I. Everybody loved him because he was a kind, generous guy. He was my first proper boyfriend—I'd always been rather lacking in confidence where men were concerned, but he made me feel I was the most beautiful girl in the world.'

Connor felt a jolt of remorse—could her lack of confidence in men have stemmed from the way he'd put her down at the school dance? Such a transient thing, but it could have been the catalyst to make her lose her self-belief. What a bastard he'd been, he reflected. However, Victoria was still talking, lost in the story of her marriage, and he listened to her intently.

'Suddenly everything in my life seemed rosy—I loved my job, and he was doing so well with every prospect of becoming a consultant.' She sighed. 'I don't know how long his affair had been going on, but it was only when a party of us were down at the beach one day and I was walking along the sand dunes that I almost literally stumbled over the two of them…'

Her voice dropped to a whisper and Connor prompted her gently. 'It must have been terrible for you.'

Victoria shrugged. 'I felt a fool. I'd had absolutely no idea what was happening, and yet I suspect some of our friends were aware of it. Our marriage had been a total sham.'

'He should have been honest and told you,' said Connor harshly. 'Even if he hadn't been sure about his sexuality, it was cruel to deceive you in that way.'

'Perhaps he thought he loved me once, but now I'm inclined to believe he married me because it would help further his career. And I know he wanted children, but in a conventional manner. Andy just wasn't brave enough to come out and say or admit to himself what he really was.' Then she added rather angrily, 'But in doing so he broke my heart—and took five years of my life away.'

'And you were thousands of miles away from home and felt especially vulnerable,' remarked Connor.

She nodded. 'That's right. So, you see, I don't think I'm a good judge of husband material, and that's why I can never take a chance on love again.'

He tilted her chin up with his hand and looked down at her strangely, his eyes traversing her face, lingering for a second on the sweep of her lashes, then focussing on her parted lips. His voice was rough. 'You know, Freckles, you've got to stop looking back. You were duped into a marriage on false promises, but you're free as a bird now—free to do anything you want. And you're not the first person this has happened to. Surely you can take a chance on fun?'

'I told you—don't call me Freckles,' she said, almost absently. 'We're not at school now.'

'No, sweetheart, we're quite grown up now, you and I.'

The flutter of butterflies started again in her stomach when he looked down at her. Those changeable eyes of his seemed full of understanding—and something else… The unmistakable hot passion of sexual attraction. His cobalt eyes locked with her tawny ones and she knew what was going to happen. Her head was spinning with so many thoughts that she did nothing to evade him when his mouth gently and sensually brushed her full lips. She stood as still as a statue and closed her eyes, feeling her body flickering into response. His tongue teased her lips open and his arms wound round her waist, pulling her towards him so that she could feel the heat of his body through his shirt. What was she doing? she thought desperately, scrabbling for some sort of self-control. Wasn't it probable that, having heard her sad little story, he thought he was onto a good thing? A woman who was obviously longing for a man to comfort her after her very sad experience had dropped neatly into his lap. After all, she was a very ordinary woman, someone who couldn't attract or keep the right kind of man.

She forced her head away from his demanding mouth and, putting her hands on his shoulders, held him at bay with all her strength.

'What the hell are you doing, Connor?' she said desperately. 'This is ridiculous! We…we mustn't behave like this.'

She looked up at him with wide tawny eyes flashing angrily, but underneath her emotions were as jumbled as ingredients in a mixing machine. How easy it would be to capitulate and enjoy a bit of casual sex to drown her sadness. But Connor and her… He was the last man on earth she should be attracted to.

And if she did allow that attraction to take over, how could she ever have a working relationship with him again?

His eyes were hot with desire, and he said roughly, 'I don't want to make you do anything you don't want to, Victoria. The trouble is, you're just too bloody attractive…' His finger traced a line from her jaw to the little hollow in her throat, fluttered over her cleavage, and he murmured, 'And, anyway, why have we got to behave well all the time? I've no doubt you and I were like paragons of virtue in our marriages—now we're not married, beholden to no one…' He gave a sudden harsh laugh. 'Why can't we have a little fun?'

Victoria drew herself up to her full height—a little difficult when Connor was about three inches away from her. 'Being married to Andy was everything to me, Connor, and I can't just jettison the memories of my marriage as lightly as you can.'

Connor looked at her strangely. 'Is that what you think— that Carol meant so little to me that I've forgotten her?'

Victoria shook her head. 'I'm sorry. Perhaps I misread the situation, but it seems to me you're just using me because I'm an available female. You always did want to dominate and have your own way…'

He dropped his arms from around her, stepped back as if she'd slapped his face and shook his head slightly. It was as if a bucket of cold water had been thrown over him, bringing him back to his senses. Was Victoria right? Was he using her because the temptation to crush her body against his was too much for his self-control after months of abstinence? After all, he sure didn't want to get involved with any female again for a long time—he wanted no commitment, although suddenly he realised he was only too happy to have sex!

He tried to look at her objectively, her slender figure and

full breasts, silky auburn hair rather tousled, and she looked back at him with her large hazel eyes. Then he felt a wave of anger. It wasn't fair to blame him entirely.

'Hell,' he growled. 'It's not just me, Victoria—there's a spark between us, and don't tell me you haven't felt that as well. We may not see eye to eye sometimes—heaven knows, you're as stubborn as a mule when you want to be—but I'm a doctor and I know a sexual response when I feel one. Like I did on the first day we worked together!'

A blush of pink spread over Victoria's cheeks. 'I don't know what you mean,' she retorted heatedly.

He laughed. 'Of course you know what I mean. Look, I'm not suggesting lifelong commitment—heaven knows, we've both been bitten once. I don't want to frighten you with any long-term entanglement. Can't we have a little fun?'

It was a chilly sensation, hearing Connor speak like that. He seemed able to think of sex without love, to propose an affair without any involvement. And yet, Victoria thought wistfully, how wonderful it was to be held in his arms, to feel her whole body come alive after all the crushing heartache of the past year—to know that someone found her attractive. But did she want that kind of casual relationship?

She shook her head firmly. 'Connor, I don't want to…'

He took her face roughly in his hands, covering her lips with his and preventing her from saying anything else.

'Is this what you don't want me to do?' he said softly, drawing back for a second. 'Tell me that you don't like it, and I won't believe you!'

Then his mouth became more demanding, teasing her lips apart and invading her mouth with a rough urgency. She gasped, not with outrage but with pleasure. The outside world started to fade, the rush of the waterfall and Buttons's lively barking becoming mere background noise. She was aware only of Connor's hard body against hers, feeling herself respond to his demands, oblivious to everything but the thrill of being desired. Her arms wound round his neck and she pressed herself to him with an enthusiasm that matched his, their bodies melting into each other. His hand slipped inside her shirt, cupping her soft breast, and she arched herself against him, feeling her insides liquefy with longing. What the hell did it matter if they did make love? This was what she needed, wasn't it?

When Connor's mobile phone began to ring it was as shocking as a gunshot—and a lifeline to sanity.

Connor groaned into her neck and swore softly. 'Wouldn't you know it?' he rasped, stepping reluctantly back from her after a few seconds and feeling in his pocket for his phone. 'Terrific timing.' He grimaced and touched her cheek apologetically, before barking into the mouthpiece, 'Yes? What is it?'

Victoria watched his eyes widen in disbelief as he listened to the caller.

'We're on our way,' he said at last, and slowly put his phone back. He turned to Victoria and said wryly, 'You're not going to believe this. There's been a huge flood at the surgery and the ceiling's come down over Reception. We'll have to get back. I'm sorry about your free afternoon, but it's an emergency and all hands literally to the pump, I think.'

He tilted her face towards his, his dark eyes looking deep into hers. 'We'll complete this episode another time, Freckles.'

We'll see about that, thought Victoria grimly, still trembling from Connor's passionate onslaught as she followed him, with Buttons bounding along the path beside her. Thank God the mobile phone had saved her on the brink of doing something extremely stupid. It had given her a moment to reflect that what was just a bit of fun to Connor had suddenly become much more than a little flirtation to her.

She stopped for a moment in her tracks, and touched her tingling lips. Suddenly she was blindingly aware that the stupid schoolgirl crush she'd once had on Connor had blossomed again. She didn't just fancy the man absolutely rotten—she wanted much more than a casual affair. She wanted commitment and affection. And that was why making love with him on a light-hearted basis was never going to be an option and why she was terrified that things would go too far, too fast.

Connor turned back to see where she'd got to and yelled, 'Come on, what are you dawdling for? The lunch-hour's over now!'

Lunch-hour? Was that all she'd been—a bit of recreation while they'd had some time off? She'd had a tremendously lucky escape, Victoria told herself furiously as she panted towards the surgery. In future she and Connor would keep their relationship on a strictly business footing—otherwise she had a feeling that her heart could be broken again.

Much of the afternoon was spent in mopping up Reception and getting hold of plumbers and electricians. Maggie and Karen had taken the full force of the water as it had cascaded through the ceiling from the fractured water tank, so they had gone home to change. Victoria and Connor decided to divide the most urgent cases between them and have two short surgeries, despite the fact that all the computers had been switched off and the only electric circuit that worked was the lights.

There was no time for either of the doctors to talk to each other, and that was for the best, thought Victoria thankfully as she waited for her next patient to lie down on the examining couch. Her relationship with Connor seemed to have changed dramatically from verbal sparring to physical contact in a most alarming manner. It was as though someone had flicked a switch and both of them had been drawn to each other like magnets to iron filings. But it was obvious from what he'd said that he didn't want to be tied down—there was no long-term future in it. Perhaps, she thought bleakly, he saw her as fair game, a lonely woman on the loose.

She snapped on the overhead light and forced herself to concentrate on palpating Alf Seddon's abdomen, which had been giving the man so much pain and nausea during the past few weeks.

'When does this tend to happen?' she asked.

Alf, a large red-faced man, considered for a moment. 'After breakfast, and nearly always after my supper. I feel terrible, quite faint.'

'What do you normally have for breakfast?'

Alf pursed his lips. 'Ooh—something fairly light. I've never wanted much first thing in the morning. Just a few rashers of fried bacon and an egg—perhaps some black pudding and a slice or two of toast.'

'And for supper?'

'Well, we usually make that the main meal of the day, so we have sausages or a steak and kidney pie, a few chips and a nice apple tart with cream, say. All good home-cooked stuff, mind—my wife never buys that ready-meal rubbish. Although as I said before, Doctor, we don't have big meals, try and keep our intake low.'

He began to put his shirt back on and sat down in front of the desk, his enormous stomach overlapping his trousers.

Victoria wondered wryly what he ate when he had what he considered a large meal. 'Well, of course, I can't be certain until we've done some tests,' she said, 'but it may be that you've some gallstones and your gall bladder's inflamed. That's the organ that processes the fats you eat.'

Her patient looked surprised. 'But surely you've got to eat a lot of fat for that to happen?'

'But your intake of fat is pretty large,' pointed out Victoria. 'Fried bacon, black pudding, chips…you must cut those out for a start.'

Alf looked almost comically dismayed. 'What shall I eat, then?'

Victoria took a piece of paper out of a drawer and handed it to him. 'There you are, Alf—a diet sheet. Stick to that and it might help you to feel better, but in the meantime I'm booking you into St Hilda's for a scan and some blood tests to see what your liver and kidney function are like. If that doesn't prove anything, then we'll book a gastroscopy and see what else it could be.'

Alf looked nervous. 'I don't like the sound of that.'

'It's all right,' said Victoria soothingly. 'They look down into your stomach with a tiny camera—they can see everything. It takes about five minutes and you'll be given a sedative so you won't be aware what's going on. The hospital will let you know when you're to go in.'

'Right,' said the man mournfully as he got up to go. 'It's a bit of a shock, all this—sounds as if I can't eat anything tasty.'

'No, Alf, I said don't eat anything fatty—you can still eat tasty foods, you know!'

'Well, thanks, Doctor…' He jerked his head towards Reception. 'You're in a right mess here, aren't you?'

He lumbered out and despite her gloomy mood Victoria grinned to herself. She wouldn't bet that Alf would stick to the diet she'd given him. She went over to the window and pulled aside the blind. It was almost dark and there was a deep red slash of sky over the woods where just a few hours ago Connor had kissed her, obliterating every bit of common sense she'd had. Perhaps, she reflected sadly, she was one of those people who took life too seriously, who couldn't regard a flirtation as lightly as he obviously could.

She sighed and dropped the blind back on the darkening night. Organising the sponsored run with Connor meant they were going to spend too much time alone together—she would have to co-opt Maggie and Karen into helping them.

She went through to Reception to call in her last patient, a little boy sitting in a Superman suit on his pregnant mother's knee.

'Harry Tate—or should I call you Superman?' She smiled. 'Will you come in now?'

When the little boy and his mother were sitting down in front of her, Victoria looked in amusement at the little boy.

'Now, Harry,' she said, picking up her otoscope, 'I believe you came to see Dr Saunders about your poor ear last week. Let me look at it with my magic light and see if it's improved at all.'

The child sat still until Victoria had finished examining him, then he said gravely, 'I'm going to be a doctor.'

'You are? Why do you want to be a doctor, Harry?'

'Because I like that torch thing you've got and that thing you use to listen inside my chest.'

Victoria caught his mother's eye and winked. 'A very good reason to be a doctor. And there are other instruments that are fun, too—like this one. We call it a sphygmomanometer and I'm going to put it on your mummy's arm now to take her blood pressure.' She looked at Jane Tate. 'May as well check you up while you're here—save you coming back for your monthly check-up next week. How are you feeling?'

'Thank you,' said Jane. 'I'm feeling vast now and doing extra journeys isn't much fun. But only another six weeks to go!'

'Are you organised for someone to look after Harry when you go into St Hilda's?' asked Victoria as she wound the cuff round Jane's arm.

'My mother's all set to do a granny dash.' Jane grinned.

'Good that she lives so near. Yes...that pressure's fine. Now, don't do too much and I'll see you next month. Harry's ear looks much better so hopefully it won't give him any more trouble.'

Victoria walked to the door with them and laughed as she watched the little boy running down to Reception, his Superman cape flying behind him.

'You know, Harry,' she exclaimed as he stopped to wait for his mother, 'you've just given me a brilliant idea. We're having a sponsored run to raise money to keep the hospital in Braithwaite. I think we should make it a fun run and get people to dress up in fancy-dress, like you are at the moment. What do you think?'

Harry looked back and gave her a gapped-tooth grin. 'I think that would be great! Daddy could go as a dinosaur!'

He looked up at his mother and they both giggled together. Watching them, Victoria felt a sudden pang of loss. She'd told Connor that it had been lucky she and Andy had never had children. That didn't mean she didn't yearn to have a child some time, and seeing a dear little boy like Harry and the sense of fun that he enjoyed with his mother made her realise just how much she was missing—and how fast the years were going by.

She finished writing up her notes on Harry and his mother, tidied up her files and put on her coat. It had been a long day with rather too much incident in it, and she couldn't wait to get back into the house and have a glass of wine by the fire. She went through to the waiting room, which was still in a mess with the chairs moved back from the area of the flood and the carpet rolled against the wall. A man was standing in Reception, wearing a tracksuit and a sweatband round his head, drumming his fingers impatiently on the counter. His muddy trainers and splattered tracksuit bottoms showed that he'd been running.

'Isn't anyone on Reception?' he asked in an aggrieved voice. 'I've been here ages.'

Victoria stopped. 'I'm afraid we've had a flood and the receptionists have gone home to dry out. The surgery's closing now.'

The man frowned and said brusquely, 'Well, I need a prescription.'

'If you come back tomorrow, it'll be ready. It is a repeat prescription, I take it?'

'Yes, but I must have it earlier than usual. Tomorrow's no good. I'm going away.'

His peremptory tone jarred, and Victoria flicked a look at the wall clock, unable to stop herself from sounding terse. 'You've left it a bit late—we're usually closed by this time anyway. It's only because of this emergency that we're still working. It's seven o'clock now. What's your name?'

'Charles Bennet. I couldn't get here earlier and this holiday's come up at the last minute.'

'You'll have to wait while I get your notes from the office.'

He frowned. 'Surely it'll only take a minute on the computer?'

'They're not working, Mr Bennet. The flood saw to that.'

'Well, will it take long? We're going out tonight and I said I'd help my wife to put the kids to bed.'

Victoria put her prescription pad down for a second. After a long day her patience was running thin. 'Mr Bennet, if it was so urgent, why didn't you come before your evening run? As I said, surgery is closed now and just because you didn't bother to order your prescription earlier, I don't have to give it you this second.'

'I'm an asthmatic—it's absolutely imperative that I have my medicine,' growled the man, his face reddening. 'You'd be failing in your duty if you refused to give it me. In fact, I'd report you.'

'Anything wrong?' Connor's deep voice floated over the waiting room.

'Nothing I can't deal with, thank you,' said Victoria tersely. 'Mr Bennet needs a 'script urgently because he's going on holiday tomorrow. I'm going to see what he needs.'

She went into the office to look at the written files and she could hear Connor say bitingly to Charles, 'It's your responsibility to let the surgery know in good time if you need a repeat prescription—you can't expect the doctors to put themselves out just because of your social life.'

Victoria grinned to herself—at least she could rely on Connor to back her up where unreasonable patients were concerned! When she came back she wrote up the prescription on her pad, tore off the page and handed it to Charles. He looked mulishly at her as he took it.

'I'm under a lot of stress,' he said sulkily. 'I need this holiday. Anyway, thanks for this.' He turned on his heel and disappeared out of the door.

'Honestly…' fumed Victoria, glaring after him. 'Talk about cheek!'

Connor started to switch the lights off and grinned at her. 'Poor chap! Remember he's under a lot of stress…'

'So am I.'

'Patients—they're a damn nuisance, aren't they?' Connor took her arm as she passed him on her way to the front door. 'No wonder you're tired—it's been quite a day. Let me make you supper.'

Victoria shook her head firmly. No way was she going to put herself in any more compromising situations with Connor. She couldn't trust him—or herself—not to let things go further.

'No, Connor, and that's definite.' She pulled her arm gently from his, her expression determined. 'I have to make it clear that any relationship we have from now on has got to be a business one. Today was…well, we seem to have slipped into another gear altogether…'

He frowned and said impatiently, 'Oh, I know all that rubbish about not getting serious—but who wants to be serious after what you and I have been through with our divorces? I'm saying it would be nice to have a…well, a light-hearted friendship. That's what we both want, isn't it?'

'No, it isn't!' snapped Victoria. 'You're making assumptions. I'm not up for jolly romps at the moment…especially with a colleague.' She folded her arms and said with determination, 'Actually, Connor, all I want from you is to have a good working relationship.'

Connor's mouth twitched slightly. 'Well, that would be a good start,' he murmured, then grinned. 'But I don't believe that's all you want.'

'Believe what you like—' she began. A terrible crash of

glass from the far end of the surgery interrupted her and made them both turn in alarm.

'What the blazes…?' Connor was off down the corridor, snapping on the lights he'd just switched off. He turned back to Victoria. 'Someone's trying to get in,' he said urgently. 'Ring the police—I'm going to see what's happening.'

'Connor…' Victoria caught his sleeve. 'Wait here—it's not safe to go yourself.'

'I told you, ring the police,' he snapped, disappearing round the corner.

It took two minutes to phone for help and then Victoria followed him, her heart hammering, suddenly feeling terrified that Connor might be harmed. There was no getting away from it—the thought of him lying maimed or worse gave her a horrible hollow feeling of loss. The building was completely silent, which in a way was more unnerving than if there'd been the sound of a fight. She peeped round the corner, half expecting Connor's lifeless body to be lying on the floor, but she was nearly knocked over by him running back towards her.

'Some damned yob was trying to get through that window,' he yelled. 'When he saw me he dropped back. I'm going after him!'

'For goodness' sake, Connor, he'll be miles away by now. Anyway, suppose he's got a knife?'

'Stay here!' was all the reply she got.

The window had been shattered by a huge stone and round the jagged hole were smears of blood, as if the intruder had tried to squeeze through or enlarge the hole with his hands. With any luck he's left a trail of blood the police can follow, thought Victoria ghoulishly. She went back to the waiting room where the front door was wide open, with no sign of

Connor, and sat down wearily on a chair. What a day! She looked around at the wrecked room, the broken ceiling and ruined carpet and almost laughed. This was something she definitely couldn't put in an email to her mother!

A few minutes later a police car arrived, just as Connor's panting figure appeared through the door.

'No sign of the blasted youth—but there's enough forensic evidence there to nail someone if they're on a police file already,' Connor said.

'We've every chance of getting them,' said the constable who'd got out of the car. 'We can narrow it down a bit to known druggies looking for a quick fix from supplies at your surgery for a start.'

'You don't need me, do you?' asked Victoria wearily. 'I really could do with a good night's rest.'

She went to the counter to pick up the prescription pad she'd left there and looked around in irritation, then closed her eyes. 'Oh, no, I might have guessed,' she groaned. 'My 'script pad's gone—that guy probably came running round to the front when he couldn't get through that window and just snatched what he could.'

'That's all we need,' growled Connor. 'We don't want forged prescriptions flying around the district. You shouldn't have left it lying around.'

Victoria put her hands on her hips and stared at him angrily, reacting over the top in her relief that the darned man was safe and the incident with the intruder was over. 'Just what do you mean by that?'

'You know what happens when these 'scripts get in the wrong hands—every druggie in the district will pay to get hold of them.'

'Excuse me! We've had a flood, I've done a surgery for you, someone's tried to burgle the place, and you're saying it's my fault the damned pad is missing?'

The constable stepped in tactfully. 'We'll get Forensics round straight away,' he promised. 'And perhaps you'd better get that window boarded up.' He gave Victoria an apprehensive glance, as if wondering if she'd explode, then walked off, speaking rapidly into his walkie-talkie.

Connor put his hands up in apology. 'OK. I was out of order again. Sorry, Victoria.'

Victoria gave him a withering look. 'You're the most contentious man I've ever met,' she snapped. 'You're always finding fault. Perhaps instead of running off to find the intruder you should have stayed here until the police arrived.'

'Perhaps you're right,' he said lightly. 'I must learn to keep my mouth shut. I admit it's been quite a gruelling end to an…active day. We're both tired.' His deep blue eyes held hers for a second with a direct message of lust in them. 'And yet some of it was pretty good earlier on…'

Victoria's cheeks reddened and she busied herself by looking for her keys in her bag, ignoring his last remark. 'We haven't decided when we should have this run yet,' she said tersely. 'I suggest we have it in two weeks' time, and I think we should make it a fun run, with people dressing up in costumes. I'm going to co-opt Pete, Maggie and the others to help.'

Connor raised an eyebrow as if he knew quite well why she was making sure there were other people involved and not just the two of them.

'That's a quick decision! OK, in two weeks it is. And by the way, I'm still going to make you a meal some time…to discuss the practice, of course!'

There were a thousand reasons why she shouldn't have a meal alone with Connor, thought Victoria, still feeling a rush of irritation at his criticism of her, mixed with thankfulness that he wasn't hurt. She ran quickly across the courtyard to the house and let herself in—but a picture of those amused blue eyes floated in her head.

From the surgery Connor watched her slim figure disappear into the house and cursed himself. Why the hell had he criticised her for being careless about the prescription pad? She was quite right. They'd had a tense few hours, what with the flood and the intruder, and she'd been a star, helping out when needed and keeping her head when that yob had tried to break in. He sighed. If only he could stop his habit of finding fault, and keep a curb on his critical tongue...

The afternoon by Daniel's Leap had taken him by surprise—he hadn't started out with any intention of kissing Victoria. Then suddenly, like a flash of lightning, it seemed that they'd been irresistibly drawn to each other, like bees to honey, and for a while he'd thought that both of them had put their sad pasts behind them. He'd glimpsed a future with a promise of something exciting, something to look forward to—a chance to wipe out the unhappiness that had dogged his life with Carol.

His feelings for Victoria seemed to be becoming more intense, and it was hard to understand because he didn't believe in happy ever after and commitment, did he? It was most odd, but he couldn't stop thinking about her. He enjoyed their verbal sparring, the undercurrent of attraction that flickered between them. Life had become exciting once more.

Connor picked up his medical bag, slipped some correspondence into it to read at home and sighed heavily. Victoria was the sexiest, most desirable woman he'd ever met, he admitted to himself in a sudden surge of honesty. But getting entangled again—was that wise? He'd learned the hard way that sex didn't lead to happiness. He flung down his bag again impatiently, and lifted the telephone to make a call to the local builders for them to come and replace the window.

CHAPTER SEVEN

'Now the surgery's back to normal after that flood, I'm putting this poster up in Reception—what do you think?'

Karen held up a large painting of a hospital with jolly figures of nurses, doctors and patients running around the building, obviously done by children. In large letters underneath were the words: 'Save St Hilda's Hospital by taking part in The Cedars' Fun Run!'

'That's fantastic, Karen. Who did it?' said Victoria in delight.

'Some of the children at Braithwaite Primary School—my kids go there and so do Lucy's. I was telling one of the teachers about the fun run and she suggested that the school should help. Quite a few of them are going to enter the race—they're really excited about it!'

'And so are some of the patients,' said Maggie. She giggled as she added, 'Those that are well enough anyway!'

Pete looked up from the computer. 'I've been on to the local press and they're sending a photographer as well as a journalist, and the WI is manning a drinks tent at the top of the field.'

'I certainly did the right thing, asking you lot to help organise the thing,' remarked Victoria. 'You're real stars, getting everything sorted so quickly. You think we'll get a lot of entries, then?'

Pete laughed. 'I should think so! Everyone seems to be flinging themselves into it—the dressing-up part has really got people's imaginations going. What are you going as, Victoria?'

Victoria looked rather nonplussed. 'I wasn't going to go in for it,' she protested. 'I'm more into the organising—like starting the thing off or something like that.'

'Absolute nonsense!'

Connor came into the office and Victoria's heart did a loop the loop at the sight of him dressed in a white T-shirt and rather ragged shorts. Her policy of trying not to think about the man, to keep a distance emotionally from him, didn't seem to be working very well! The trouble was his tanned, muscled legs and broad shoulders made it too easy for her mind flip back to Daniel's Leap and the way he'd wrapped his arms around her, his hard body pressing against hers.

It was no good longing for that, she told herself crossly. He'd told her he wasn't up for a committed relationship, and at least that was honest. If only she'd realised that Andy's love for her had been a sham—the conventional behaviour he believed was necessary for his ambitions.

Connor's eyes ranged over her sternly. 'You've got to set an example—as all of you have,' he declared. 'I'm training for it. I've just done the circuit now before work…'

'Wow!' exclaimed Karen. 'You turn up like that for surgery and every woman in the practice will be putting her name down to run!'

He grinned. 'Put them off more like. But, seriously, it would do you all good to get out every morning.'

'Oh, yes?' said Maggie sarcastically. 'And who's going to

take my kids to school, walk the dog and clear up the dishes if I'm to start pounding round circuits before I start here in the morning?'

Connor's blue eyes twinkled. 'Now you're just making excuses! You can run round the field in the lunch-hour!'

'Not in these heels,' grumbled Maggie.

Everyone laughed and Victoria felt a sense of pleasure in the feeling that the staff in the practice was so committed to making the event they were organising a success. Outside was another poster that Connor had made up with a huge photograph of St Hilda's and another one of a supermarket with the words 'Which would you rather have serving the community?' and an invitation for people to put their names down to take part in the event. There were a heartening number of signatures at the bottom.

'We'll outdo every other fundraising event, I'm sure of it,' declared Karen. 'And we've got a week to decide what we're all going as. I've already got St John's Ambulance booked in case of any casualties.'

Victoria went to her room to open her post, satisfied that things were going well for the fun run. She'd brought letters across with her from the house to save time, and there were some from the estate agents she'd contacted about looking at houses. She quickly riffled through them and, having seen one or two that interested her, put them on one side to organise viewings later on.

Amongst the letters was one from Social Services saying that Mrs Gelevska and her children ought to be moved and that they would be a priority on the housing list, but that there was nothing suitable at the moment. They also added that Evie was taking time off school in order to look after her mother and that this was unacceptable. They would try and arrange for someone to at least do the shopping for Evie and her mother.

'But when?' Victoria asked herself. 'It could be months…'

'Talking to yourself? You know what that's the first sign of, don't you?' Connor put his head round the door. 'All right to come in for a minute?'

'No wonder I'm talking to myself,' said Victoria, sighing. 'I haven't got much further with Evie Gelevska and her mother. There's nothing available in the housing line for them, and I have a horrible feeling Social Services might interfere rather too much when it comes to Evie not attending school.'

Connor sat down on the edge of her desk, still dressed in his old shorts, his tanned and bare muscular legs on the floor about a foot away from her. Victoria ignored the prickling sensation at the back of her neck at his proximity and took a sip of water from the glass on her desk, looking studiously at the letter.

'Are you worried she might be taken into care?' queried Connor.

Victoria sighed. 'I promised them there'd be no question of that, and I'll feel terrible if that happens.'

'You'd think there'd be somewhere better than that shell of a place they're living in at the moment—lovely though the scenery is.'

'I'll ring up Social Services and talk to them again. There may be private places to let in the village which, although they're small, would suit the Gelevskas… Which reminds me, I'm going to be looking at estate agents' windows myself later today—I need to find a place of my own. You realise that John and my mother will be back soon and they'll presumably want to live in one of their homes?'

'I'll make a guess that it's your mother's house they'll

want. My father's flat's very basic so he'll probably sell it and I'll be on the hunt for somewhere. I wouldn't want to live there permanently.'

'Your father used to live in a big house about five miles away, didn't he?'

A wry smile crossed Connor's face. 'He thought there'd be plenty of room for grandchildren, but when none arrived he got tired of living so far out and chose somewhere he could look after easily and was more convenient.'

Victoria looked at Connor thoughtfully. 'So the flat will be on the market, then?'

'I imagine so—no point in hanging on to it—but I'll have to wait until he comes back.'

'It might be quite a good investment to hang on to, don't you think?'

'Could be. Why?'

'I was thinking of Evie and her mother and little brother actually—it would be ideal for them.'

Connor looked quizzically at her. 'Ah, now I see the interest in my father's property...all for the sake of your patients!'

'So what?' said Victoria boldly. 'It would be a nice little earner for him, and it would be helping the Gelevskas out of a difficult hole.'

'Nevertheless, I can't see my father wanting to let it.'

A stubborn expression crossed Victoria's face. 'You haven't asked him yet.'

Connor leant back on the desk and grinned at her. 'You don't give up easily, do you? It does need a lot throwing out, though. As I told you, there's old stuff from the surgery that's been stored there that you might want to look over before it's chucked out. You ought to come and see if it's suitable for the Gelevskas.'

'Perhaps,' said Victoria cautiously.

'Tell you what—if you'll allow me to make dinner for you in that very flat, I'll see what I can do about asking my father.'

'That's blackmail.' Victoria's eyes locked with his for a second. 'I told you I didn't think it was a good idea for us to…to socialise together.'

'For God's sake, Victoria, what baloney! I don't know what you're frightened of. We're two grown people who happen to work together. Why does that stop us having a friendly relationship—not just work based?'

Even as he said it, Connor wondered if Victoria was right—perhaps having her round on her own wasn't a good idea. His eyes flicked over her in her decorous work suit—navy blue with a clear-cut line that emphasised her full breasts and neat waist, the knee-length skirt revealing long slender legs. Who wouldn't be attracted to someone like her? Then he reflected bitterly that that was what had hooked him into Carol's orbit—the sex appeal of a beautiful woman—and he wasn't about to make that mistake again.

He snapped back to reality as Victoria's cool voice broke into his thoughts.

'As long as it's just friendship you want,' she said lightly, 'perhaps you think I'm being stuffy, but I've just come out of one disastrous relationship…'

Her voice trailed off, because what she'd really meant was that if she wasn't careful she'd fall hook, line and sinker for this man and it was going to be difficult to keep any relationship they had light and friendly. Another intimate setting, a little wine and her longing to feel his arms around her again might get the better of her!

An unreadable expression flitted briefly across Connor's

face and he sighed. 'Far be it from me to suggest lifelong commitment. I've done the happy-ever-after bit—believed that Carol and I would weather the storms and be together for ever.' Then he added softly, 'But surely our pasts don't stop us from being friends.'

Victoria was silent for a minute. Was she to be lonely for the rest of her life, rejecting any friendship from men because she might fall for them? It was fear that prevented her from taking any chances—fear that she'd be taken for a ride again by an opportunistic male. Then suddenly she felt acute anger that she was allowing Andy and what he'd done to her dictate what her future life would be like. She sprang up from the desk, and went over to the window and turned round to face Connor, her arms folded.

'When would this dinner be?' she said carefully.

'Whenever you like—tomorrow night? And seeing you're so incredibly worried about being alone with me, I promise it will be a strictly friendly meeting.' His eyes sought hers for a second. 'Absolutely nothing physical… As I've mentioned before, there are some things in the flat that used to be in the surgery—you could look through them and decide if we need to keep anything.'

He swung his legs down from the desk and stretched. 'I'll go and put some clothes back on now. As Karen said, I don't want to excite my patients too much.'

Victoria laughed. 'Talk about conceited!'

'Don't tell me you don't like me in these shorts,' he retorted as he went out of the door.

He went straight to his room and sat down in front of his desk, staring unseeingly for a minute at the graphics dancing around on the screen of his computer. Then he gave a wry grin.

All his good advice to Victoria about not allowing her broken marriage to dictate her life now might actually apply to him as well! Carol had been a strong woman. Both she and Victoria were feisty characters, but Victoria was driven by compassion, not greed and self-regard, so why be so frightened of getting involved with her?

Thoughtfully he punched a key on the keyboard and brought up the name of his first patient.

Maggie knocked on Victoria's door and came in, holding something in her hand. 'I've found that prescription pad you told me someone had stolen,' she said.

'What? That's amazing. It's been missing for ages! Where did you find it?'

Maggie looked at her with barely concealed triumph. 'Your next patient's pocket,' she said. 'He's got one of those duffle coats on with a hood. The pockets are stuffed full of rubbish and when he pulled out his handkerchief by the desk, the pad flew out and onto the counter—I recognised it immediately! The daft idiot said he'd just found it and was about to hand it in—as if! Mind you, I didn't say anything.'

'Well done, you. What's his name?'

'Brett Canfield—he's a bit of a lad around these parts.'

Victoria frowned. 'That rings a bell… Send him in.'

As soon as she saw the youth slouching into the room Victoria recognised him, although the last time she'd seen him had been several weeks ago on her first day in the practice. It had been pouring with rain and there had been a terrible accident outside the pub—the boy before her was the driver of one of the crashed cars.

'Hello, Brett,' she said calmly. 'How can I help you this time?'

He scowled and thrust his arm at her. 'Cut meself, see? Only it seems to get worse instead of better.'

Victoria looked at the jagged tear in his arm. 'How did you do this, Brett?' she asked, holding his gaze with stony eyes.

He shifted uneasily on his dirty trainers. 'Just cut it…'

'On glass perhaps?' Victoria got up from her chair and went round the desk so that she was standing directly in front of him. 'You tried to get into the surgery through the window last week, didn't you?'

The boy started to protest and Victoria put up her hand to silence him. 'Don't deny it, Brett. The police have got your DNA from the blood you left on the broken window so it's going to be so easy to prove. Not to mention the prescription pad in your pocket—stolen from here last week.'

'So, you going to grass on me?' he muttered.

'You're going to give yourself up to the police,' said Victoria tersely. 'If you don't, I will report you. I'm giving you a chance to help yourself. Now, let me look at this arm.'

She took his arm and looked at it closely, noting the suppuration of the weeping cut and, below that, several needle-puncture marks.

'This is badly infected—you'll need antibiotics,' she said. 'I'm going to ask the practice nurse to dress it before you go and you must finish the course of the pills.' She looked up at him. 'Why do you do these stupid things, Brett? Mind you, I think I know the answer.' She pointed to the punctures on his arm.

Brett avoided her eyes and muttered something unintelligible.

'Why don't you let us help you? I know you're on drugs… You're always dropping things out of those pockets of yours. Today you dropped my prescription pad, and when you had the car crash a few weeks ago a small packet of cocaine fell out of your pocket. I was told by the hospital that they put you on a course of rehab. Did you give up?'

He looked at her bleakly, then unexpectedly burst into tears, rubbing his eyes with his knuckles and sniffling pathetically. 'I…I'm sorry, miss. I did try—but a mate offered me some more and I gave in. Can you give me some more? I'll stick to it this time, I promise.'

Victoria shook her head. 'We don't keep any drugs of that nature here, Brett—that's why it was pointless for you to try and get in, if that's what you were after. I'll refer you to the drug rehab unit in Braithwaite—they'll do their best to help you.'

He kicked the side of the desk disconsolately. 'Why don't you keep them?'

'Because it needs a specialist unit to deal with this problem—people who've been trained, people who can give you continuity of care. You will go, won't you, Brett? Make a fresh start?'

'Maybe…' He got up and hoisted his hood over his head. 'So where is this nurse I go to for my dressing?'

Victoria handed him the prescription for antibiotics and directed him to the treatment room. 'And don't forget you've two places to go—to the police to admit to that break-in here and the rehab unit. Don't forget!'

She watched him slouch out and sighed. She didn't think there was much chance that he'd turn over a new leaf, although he had at least said he wanted to stick to a rehab programme, which was a start. She pressed the switch for her next patient to be shown on the screen in the waiting room. It was going to be another busy day, and tomorrow there would be her evening with Connor to get through. She gave a shiver of apprehension, mixed with a kind of nervous excitement.

* * *

The flat where Connor lived was on the ground floor of con-verted stables in a pretty mews courtyard, each section with a tiny garden surrounded by miniature palings. It was just off the main street and would, thought Victoria as she rang the bell, be absolutely ideal for Mrs Gelevska with no stairs to climb and very little distance to the shops—besides being near the school.

Connor opened the door dressed in jeans and an open-necked blue shirt. 'Come in.' He smiled.

Victoria couldn't help adding in her mind, Said the spider to the fly... If only he wasn't so good-looking, exuding sexiness from every pore, and if only she could trust herself to regard him as just a work colleague!

'You look good,' he remarked, stepping back for her to go in first and flicking a glance over the pink sweater, black chiffon scarf and cropped trousers she was wearing.

Victoria frowned as if to warn him he was treading on dan-gerous ground, and sat down on the small sofa.

'By the way,' she remarked coolly, 'that prescription pad I lost has turned up in the pocket of a young patient. He came in with an infected cut on his arm, sustained when he tried to get in through the surgery window.'

Connor raised his brows. 'Ah, so it *was* stolen. At least you've got it back. Have you informed the police?'

'It's being sorted out,' Victoria said shortly.

He nodded. 'Good. First things first... Some chilled Chablis?'

'That would be lovely,' she said, trying to force herself to relax and be natural, less aware of Connor and his drop-dead gorgeous looks.

She looked around the little sitting room of the flat while Connor was in the kitchen. It was cosy but very cluttered, with family photographs on the mantelpiece, a bookcase crammed with books and a desk overflowing with papers. Rather tarnished silver cups were arrayed on a shelf, the evidence of sporting triumphs, and a bag of golf clubs was propped against a cupboard.

She wandered over to look at the photographs, her eye drawn to one in particular, pushed behind the others. It showed a newly married couple outside a church, a cloud of confetti showering down on them. The bride was laughing up at her groom, and he was looking proudly down at her. The bride's blonde hair was swept up in a chignon, revealing a long graceful neck, and her white dress was fitted to a curvaceous figure. She was very beautiful and the groom she was looking at so lovingly was Connor. What had gone wrong with their marriage? wondered Victoria. They looked like the perfect married couple.

She stepped back from the cabinet when Connor came back with the bottle of wine, which he opened and poured into two glasses. He handed one to Victoria and smiled at her, gesturing with a sweep of his arm round the room.

'None of this is mine but, as you can see, my father likes to live in a bit of chaos. He goes mad if anyone tries to tidy up. The funny thing is, his room at the surgery was absolutely immaculate.'

'He hasn't left much room for you to spread yourself out,' remarked Victoria. She looked at some framed certificates on the top of a display cabinet. 'Ah, so you did actually qualify! Your father's obviously very proud of you—there must be every certificate you ever gained here. And are those your silver cups on that shelf?'

'No—those are Dad's. He was a great runner in his day.

Anyway, perhaps you can see why Betty might prefer to stay in her own house than squeeze in here.' He looked enquiringly at Victoria. 'Have you had any luck looking for a house yourself?'

Victoria shook her head. 'I looked at two last night after work, but I want something nearer the country—but smaller than The Cedars, of course. However, it's early days yet.'

Connor took a sip of wine and said casually, 'By the way, I emailed my father about letting the flat.'

'You did? What did he say?'

'Marriage to Betty must have softened him. He was in a good mood, because he said if I could get a reasonable rate he was happy to let it. Do you think the Gelevskas could get help with the rent?'

A broad smile lit Victoria's face. 'That's brilliant! And, yes, I'll have a word with Social Services and it might be they can arrange something.'

'Of course, this could be a great help in your search for a place,' he remarked. 'Have you ever thought that the Gelevskas' cottage might suit you?'

Victoria's eyes widened. 'No…not really. It needs to be completely regutted anyway.' She stopped for a moment, considering his remarks, then said slowly, 'It is in the most perfect position, though, and it would be fun to do up… Do you think there's any chance?'

Connor shrugged. 'We could find out if the owner's willing to sell it.'

'Perhaps it seems opportunistic,' said Victoria uneasily. 'I would hate Evie and her mother to think I was just trying to get them out so I could take advantage of the situation.'

'I'm sure they can see the sense in getting somewhere nearer the village. They're completely isolated where they are.

Mrs Gelevska's arthritis can only get worse over time, even if we manage to control it at the moment.'

A rising exhilaration with the idea began to flood Victoria's mind. It would be ideal for her—so near the surgery and yet a decent distance away from her mother and new stepfather!

'It...it would be absolutely perfect,' she admitted slowly, the notion of the little cottage in its idyllic surroundings becoming more and more attractive. She could have such fun doing it up, taming the little garden, perhaps making the windows bigger so that she could look out on those stunning views over the woods and moors.

She looked at Connor with shining eyes as he came over to fill her glass again—it would be something to look forward to, her own little home. He smiled at her delight.

'You're a genius to think of that!' she exclaimed. 'What a wonderful idea! Thank you for thinking of something so perfect!'

He bent over her shoulder to pour out more wine, and before she could stop herself she had nearly pecked his cheek in an enthusiastic demonstration of her pleasure. She drew back at the last moment, and Connor raised a sardonic eyebrow.

'I thought that wasn't allowed,' he murmured, stopping in the middle of pouring the wine and standing just a few inches away from her, a hint of mocking laughter dancing in his eyes. Victoria's face burned with embarrassment as their eyes locked. God, just how stupid could she get? Once again she'd acted without thinking.

She said in a gabbled tone, trying to hide her discomfort, 'To be honest, much as I love The Cedars, it doesn't seem like my home now. It's filled with mementos of my youth—photos of me as a little girl, a teenager, a graduate... As you said before, it's time to move on, and this would be the perfect way I could do that. That cottage has to be ideal.'

There was a 'ping' from the kitchen and Connor tilted his head. 'Sounds like supper's ready,' he said. 'It's nothing too sophisticated. Come and sit at the table here.'

'It smells tantalising,' commented Victoria, sitting down at a small table in the corner, which had a vase of freesias on it and beside it two wineglasses. Two small candles gave a glow in the dimly lit area. She unfolded a linen napkin, unaccountably touched by the amount of trouble Connor had gone to but still feeling embarrassed by that kiss she'd nearly given him.

He came across with a plate of spaghetti Bolognese and put it down before her with a slight bow. '*Voilà!* Help yourself to the salad and enjoy…'

'This looks so good, Connor, and I'm really hungry…'

He nodded approvingly as he sat down opposite her. 'Good. I'm sick of hearing about diets. Food should be enjoyed—in good company if possible.'

For a few moments they ate in silence, although quietly in the background Victoria was aware that a CD was playing some Neopolitan love songs. This, together with the flickering candlelight, made the atmosphere in the small room seem intimate, cosy—and romantic, thought Victoria nervously. She drank a quick gulp of the sparkling white wine.

'You asked me if I missed Australia,' she said at last. 'What about you—do you miss Glasgow? I know it's a really humming city with plenty to do. Braithwaite must seem rather dull after that.'

Connor refilled her glass and shrugged. 'I do love Glasgow,' he admitted, 'but my memories of it latterly aren't too great—and I love the beauty and tranquillity of the country around here.' He paused for a moment, twirling the wineglass in his fingers, and smiled into her eyes. 'And I'm growing to like my workmates quite a lot…'

Victoria felt her face burn, suddenly frightened by the desire she saw in his gaze. The tension between them had heightened again and she looked down at her plate, apparently intent in chasing a small bit of spaghetti with her fork. Her imagination was working overtime and she could almost feel his lips on hers, his hands stroking her body, and the familiar turmoil of fear, panic and excitement raced through her. It was like a reflex action when he looked at her like that.

She put down her knife and fork, a hollow feeling of despair creeping over her. She must be mad to think she could continue to work with Connor and suppress her feelings for him. In her mind's eye she saw herself many years on, trying to pretend that she didn't go weak at the knees when he was near her—it would be an impossible situation for her. He wanted a light romance after an unhappy marriage, and she would always be low on his list of priorities. She had to realise that her feelings for Connor would never be fulfilled by him committing to marriage. She'd wasted five years of her life with Andy—she couldn't waste any more years waiting for Connor.

Suddenly the feeling that she must make a decision about her future immediately overwhelmed her. She stood up, pushing her chair away. Connor looked at her in surprise.

'Had enough?' he asked.

Victoria nodded, a lump like lead in her throat. 'Yes, Connor, I've had enough. I don't mean the meal—it was delicious. I have a confession to make…'

He looked at her enquiringly, deep blue eyes holding hers. 'So?'

'Perhaps the cottage is a bad idea after all—perhaps even staying here isn't so wise. The thing is…I think I should look for another job, move away altogether, where you and I can no longer meet.'

He looked at her in astonishment, then said roughly, 'What the hell do you mean—look for another job?'

She bit her lip and thought savagely, I mean that I'm bloody well falling for you, you stupid man, and I don't want to!

To him she merely said, 'You and I want different things from each other, Connor. I shall leave as soon as we've got a locum to fill in for me.'

CHAPTER EIGHT

A CLOCK on the wall ticked loudly, the coffee bubbled in the percolator—background noises which Victoria was hardly aware of as Connor stared at her in anger and shock.

At last he said slowly, his eyes like chips of blue ice, 'You want to leave me in the lurch just as we're beginning to get used to working together in the practice? That's utterly ridiculous, and damned unprincipled,' he added acidly.

Victoria was silent and watched him as he ran a hand distractedly through his thick hair so that it stood up spikily around his forehead. He began to pace up and down the small room. She felt guilty for landing him in a difficult situation, but it was her sanity and future she was trying to protect, even though the thought of not seeing him again was horrible.

I need you! she wanted to cry, suddenly realising how empty her life was going to be and how she longed for him to make love to her. She wanted to be the main part of his life for ever, but she was damned if she'd just be his bit on the side.

'And how long has this been part of your plan?' he asked coldly. 'It seems to me it's happened pretty quickly.'

She took a deep breath. 'When we kissed each other at

Daniel's Leap that afternoon I realised that it probably meant more to me than it did to you.'

His expression changed and he said in a gentler voice, 'It was wonderful. I shall never forget it.'

But you wouldn't let it interfere with your freedom, thought Victoria sadly.

He looked down at her with those wonderful eyes holding hers, a surprisingly wistful look in their depths. 'Can't I change your mind, Freckles? Surely you're being far too hasty. We make a good medical team, it's a good practice…'

'No,' she said harshly. 'I absolutely mean to go.'

He shook his head as if bewildered and shrugged rather helplessly. 'So this is goodbye, then, is it? And will you miss me at all?'

Her voice was slightly muffled. 'Yes! Of course I'll damn well miss you!'

The little room seemed to pulse with emotion, and after a few seconds she added softly, 'And I've made another decision…'

'Don't you think you've made enough decisions for the time being?' he asked wryly.

She stepped up close to him and put her arms on his shoulders, her wide eyes looking into his. 'I want you to make love to me before I go—proper, passionate love, Connor.'

Disbelief crossed his face and he gazed at her in amazed silence for a moment, then he laughed shortly. 'Is this for real? I thought…'

She put her finger on his lips. 'Perhaps I'm mad. All I know is, if we don't make love now I shall always wonder what I missed. And besides,' she said wistfully, 'I realise that Andy didn't really fancy me—it was all a sham. I want to know what it's like to be made love to by someone who likes women!'

He shook his head in mystification. 'I can't pretend to understand you, honey. First you say you never want to see me again and now you want me to make love to you…'

Victoria nodded calmly. 'Yes, that's right. A sort of good-bye present if you like.'

'Bloody hell,' he said softly. Then he shook his head. 'I'm not a complete heel, you know. I can't take advantage of you—go to bed with you—and then never see you again.'

She held his face in her hands and pressed her cheek close to his. 'I want you to, Connor,' she whispered in his ear. 'I'll be leaving in a few days and this is the right time. I know what I'm doing.'

'Are you quite sure about this?'

She nodded and a slow grin spread over his face. He held her shoulders gently, looking down at her with those penetrating blue eyes.

'Then what are we waiting for, sweetheart?' he asked.

He drew her towards him gently but firmly and a thousand butterflies fluttered somewhere in her stomach and her heart beat a mad tattoo on her chest wall.

Gently he brushed her lips with his, then his kisses became more insistent, fiercer against her pliable mouth, teasing it open, feeling her body arch against his, her soft breasts pressed to his hard frame and her arms wound around his neck as every nerve in her body responded to his urgent demands.

'My God, Victoria,' he said thickly, 'I want you so much, sweetheart. I don't want to say goodbye to you, but if I can't persuade you to stay, then let me say goodbye properly…'

He looked intently down at her as if he could decipher the complicated emotions that were going on in her head. A feeling of release swept through Victoria, as if the past had been blown away and at last she could look to the future, stop pretending that all she wanted was a working relationship with Connor and admit that, although there was no future in it, she loved him.

'So let's make up for lost time, shall we?' she whispered, and, throwing all inhibitions away, started to undo the buttons on his blue shirt.

He gave a low chuckle and, picking her up in his arms, carried her through to his bedroom. 'I don't often get an invitation like this, my sweet. And I can't tell you how often I've wanted to make love to you,' he murmured, laying her down gently on the bed.

They looked at each other for a moment, drowning in each other's gaze, then Connor said with a grin, 'I'm going to need some help here. I don't want to rip your clothes as I tear them off…'

Victoria giggled and wriggled out of her cropped trousers and pink sweater until she lay on the bed wearing nothing more than the black chiffon scarf round her neck, part of her mind amazed at her lack of inhibition. Her tousled hair spread over the pillows, her cheeks flushed, and she looked up at him with sudden nervousness.

'Andy…well, he was the only one before you and that was a long time ago… I'm not very sure…'

Connor bent his head and kissed her with tender gentleness. 'Don't worry, sweetheart, we'll take it slowly,' he said huskily. Then he gazed down at her in wonder and stroked back her hair from her brow. 'My God, Dr Curtis,' he whispered. 'How beautiful you are!'

His hands gently traced the soft curves of her body, then he gradually lowered himself onto her, so that she felt the astonishing silkiness of their naked skin together, the hardness of his muscled body.

'Why did we take so long to do this?' he murmured into her neck.

She laughed throatily as she wrapped her body round his and his fingers ran through her hair and then over her soft curves with surprising gentleness.

'The best things are worth waiting for, aren't they?' she whispered, savouring the sweetness of their physical closeness, feeling a new and surprising power in her ability to please him.

He laughed, looking down into her eyes. 'Then let's see what we've been missing,' he murmured.

Then their limbs entwined and they lost themselves in each other, revelling in the fire of each other's passion. And Victoria knew that she would remember how Connor gave her his 'goodbye gift' for ever.

The sun filtered through the curtains, throwing light onto the outline of a wardrobe and a small dressing-table. Victoria opened her eyes wide and turned to look at Connor's sleeping figure next to her. Gently she wriggled from under his arm, which he'd curled round her body as they'd slept, then she slid from the bed and groped on the floor for her clothes.

Had she been completely mad to ask Conner to make love to her? She looked across at his profile, schoolboyish in sleep, hair tousled, mouth slightly open. No, she thought firmly, it had been a wonderful wild night of passion and, on her side at least, of love. He had been so tender, so gentle and reassuring, and then so powerful in his love-making that she could almost think that he truly loved her in return.

She sighed to herself. She wasn't so naïve as to believe that the night had meant as much to him as it had to her. He had made it memorable. She would never forget it, but it had been a 'good-bye gift' and that was all.

Victoria stood at the back of the medical centre and looked in amazement at all the people gathered on the field for the sponsored fun run, marvelling at the support they'd had from the local population. She should have been feeling on top of the world, enjoying the whole thing and the way it had been organised. Actually, she felt terrible, wondering how she would get through the next few days until a locum had been engaged to take her place. She seemed to be making a habit of moving on and having fresh beginnings, she thought sadly.

She glanced across at Connor, who was standing near the front dressed as a surgeon in hospital greens and a mask, and her lips curved in a wistful smile. She would never forget the night of love-making she'd had with him, but she knew she was doing the right thing to leave. She was making a clean break, not plodding through work here, nurturing a hopeless love for him when she knew he was not up for commitment. She quickly turned away when his eyes caught hers over the crowd and made her way over to Maggie, who was trying to sort everyone out.

Connor watched Victoria's tall slim figure disappear into the melee of people. He was oblivious to a man standing beside him giving a detailed description of a new car he'd bought. Connor couldn't stop thinking about Victoria—the way she looked, the way she talked, the way she laughed—and, of course, the way they'd made love the other night. It had been so unexpected, so unlike any other time he'd taken a woman in his arms. She had been so uninhibited, so giving in her love-making…so unlike Carol, he thought grimly. In Carol's eyes sex had had to be earned—a reward for good behaviour. His mouth twisted bitterly. Making love to his ex-wife had been a joyless affair in which she had not taken much part. But Victoria… God, he thought, it had been the most wonderful experience of his life. And why the hell was she leaving?

He jumped as the man standing next to him punched him lightly on the chest and finished his conversation. 'So what do you think, Connor? I went for the leather seats, and Gloria said she didn't like them! Women!'

Connor sighed. 'Women indeed,' he murmured.

A blast of a whistle took Victoria's attention and she turned to the starting line where a motley array of people dressed as clowns, princesses and animals were milling about. The photographer from the local paper was busy snapping everyone and to her surprise Victoria spotted Janet Loxton pushing her father Bernard in a wheelchair. She came over to Victoria looking rather embarrassed.

'Dr Curtis, just before you start, my father's got something to say to you.' She bent down towards her father and said loudly into his ear, 'Dad, tell Dr Curtis what you've got in mind.'

The old man peered up at Victoria. 'Apparently you're all dressed up in these ridiculous outfits to raise money for St Hilda's. I'd like to help a little, and as I can't run any more I'll give you one of my paintings to auction. It might help in a small way.'

Victoria gaped at them both in surprise. 'One of your paintings, Mr Lamont? That…that's fantastic…and very generous. I don't know how to thank you.'

Bernard shook his head and growled, 'It might not fetch much money, you know. Anyway, Janet and you can organise that between you.'

Janet smiled at Victoria. She looked a very different woman from the nervous and brusque patient who had come in that first day.

'I'm really grateful to you for organising that respite care at St Hilda's,' she said. 'I feel so much better for the break—and I think my father has enjoyed being away from me for a while,' she added with a rueful smile. 'We both want to support the fundraising for the hospital, and donating one of my father's paintings to auction seemed a good way to express our thanks.'

Victoria watched her push her father away, bending down to whisper something to him and then laughing at his reply. It was amazing how everyone seemed to have come together to help in the venture, and Bernard's offer would probably raise thousands of pounds. She remembered Connor telling her that there was a gallery in Glasgow devoted to his work and that anything by him was very popular.

Karen bustled in front of everyone, impressively attired as a large yellow and black bee.

'All the children and the grown-ups running with them must wait until the fast runners have gone first—we don't want anyone bowled over!' she called out. 'Maggie Brown, our receptionist, will blow the whistle to start us off.'

'How on earth did Maggie manage to wriggle out of running?' asked Pete in a muffled voice. He looked very uncomfortable with a dragon's head pulled over his own head and a tight costume of scales over his large body. 'I don't think I'll be able to run a yard in this outfit,' he added gloomily. He looked admiringly at Victoria. 'You look wonderful—are you the green goddess?'

'It was the only thing I could think of—a green Lycra suit,' said Victoria dispiritedly.

Maggie bustled up and looked defiantly at them both. 'I'm not running because of, er, medical reasons,' she said firmly. She put the whistle to her lips. 'Everyone ready? Right—here we go!'

She gave a long blast on her whistle and the group moved off raggedly.

Thankfully it was another lovely autumn day, sunlight dappling the bare trees and a crisp nip in the air—perfect for running. Connor was one of the first of the crowd, his tall figure striding out, looking like the Pied Piper with everyone following him. As they ran past the Gelevskas' cottage Victoria saw Evie, her mother and little brother at the gate, waving at them. They looked happy and smiling, probably looking forward to an easier life nearer the village now they'd learned that they were moving into the flat.

Victoria ran with the crowd through the wood and past the waterfall at Daniel's Leap where Connor had kissed her and she had begun to realise just how much she cared for him. She felt a quick flash of sadness and loss, then put her head down and pounded on resolutely. Life wasn't like a book with a happy ending—she was one of those women who needed to commit to a man. She'd just have to revise her ideas.

She had nearly caught up with Pete, his dragon's head bobbing up and down and looking comical on his lumbering burly figure. She waved at him as she overtook him, and he gave her a thumbs-up. He didn't notice the stray dog that raced in front of him as he began to run down the steps on the other side of the bridge. There was a sickening thud as he tripped over the dog and slid down to the ground. Victoria heard the yelp of the dog as Pete's substantial weight landed on it and then a yell and a forcible oath from Pete. She skidded to a halt and turned back to the incongruous figure with a dragon's head lying on the ground.

'Pete! You poor man. Are you all right?'

Pete sat up with difficulty and grimaced as he felt his ankle gingerly. 'I think I've twisted something. Can you help me off with this damned dragon's head?'

A small crowd of runners had gathered around him and Victoria waved them away. 'Go on, everyone, I can manage. You get on with your running.'

She felt in the belt of the Lycra suit for her mobile—if she needed help she could phone the surgery. She dropped down beside Pete and helped him take off the dragon's head, from whence his face appeared, red and perspiring.

'Let's look at this ankle,' she said, peeling back his track-suit bottoms, disguised with cardboard scales. Even now the ankle was swelling and turning alarmingly purple, and she decided to leave the trainer on until it could be cut off.

Pete drew in his breath sharply. 'Have I broken it?' he groaned. 'It feels terrible.'

'I don't know. To be honest, it needs an X-ray, and I don't want to be gloomy but if you haven't cracked a bone, it looks like some badly torn ligaments. You won't be running again for some time—and you certainly can't put weight on it at the moment.'

Victoria looked round and saw Karen in her bee costume pounding towards them.

'What's happened?' enquired Karen with concern. 'Don't say the dragon's been floored!'

'My own stupid fault,' said Pete, sighing. 'I should have

been concentrating. A dog ran between my legs and I fell over like a ton of bricks.'

Karen grimaced. 'Poor old you. What bad luck. The sooner you get some ice on that to reduce the swelling, the better—and a compression bandage.'

'We must treat it as a fracture just in case he's broken a bone,' added Victoria. 'In any case, he's going to need transport to St Hilda's for an X-ray. I think it's probable he's torn some ligaments in his ankle, but we can't be sure. I'd better phone for an ambulance.'

'I'm supposed to be going to this marvellous concert in York tomorrow,' Pete said dolefully.

Victoria flipped open her mobile phone but before she could dial the emergency number they heard a car coming towards them up the field towards the river. It pulled up just beside them and Connor leapt out, still attired in his surgeon's outfit. Maggie tried to suppress a giggle because Connor looked like some TV hero in a hospital soap.

'Doctor to the rescue,' she said gaily, then turned guiltily to Pete. 'Sorry, Pete, I know it's not a laughing matter, but Connor does look dressed for the part, doesn't he?'

Pete gave a weak smile. 'Superman,' he murmured.

'Hello, there,' said Connor, kneeling down beside them. 'I was back at the surgery when some of the runners came in and told me Pete had bitten the dust. I told the St John Ambulance people that I was happy to come out. What's wrong?'

'I think it's a very bad sprain,' said Victoria, 'but, of course, it needs an X-ray.'

Connor looked at Pete's injury and nodded. 'You're right, it's not very nice—a lot of contusion. Never mind, we'll get you to St Hilda's asap. You can sit in the back of the car and

I'll put the front seat down so you can prop your leg up on it.' He looked up at Victoria and said steadily, 'Perhaps Victoria would sit beside you in the back.'

Victoria's heart did a rapid tattoo on her ribs—it was too cruel to have to sit so near him. She nodded reluctantly and Connor went to bring the car as close as possible to Pete, then practically lifted him into the back seat.

'I said I'd run for St Hilda's—I didn't think I'd be using their facilities,' Pete said wryly.

When they arrived at the hospital Victoria ran inside and got a wheelchair for him, causing a certain amount of hilarity from the desk staff when they saw her outfit.

Fortunately the A and E department was relatively empty—Saturday lunchtime was too early for the drunks and football injuries that usually came in later in the day. Connor and Victoria waited rather self-consciously on a bench in the waiting room while Pete had his X-ray. She was painfully aware of being as close to Connor as they had been in bed. She stared down at the little golden hairs growing on the back of his hand—the hand that a few nights ago had caressed her so gently. It was as if it had been a dream now, but she still didn't regret a moment of it.

'I think we're causing rather a stir,' she said at last, to break the silence. 'They must wonder what a surgeon in full regalia is doing sitting with the Green Goddess!'

Connor turned round to look at her. 'Are you still adamant about leaving the practice?' he asked abruptly.

'Yes, of course I am.'

Connor shook his head. 'I don't understand you—a great job in a lovely place...' His eyes looked troubled. 'And something else—didn't the other night mean anything to you at all?'

Victoria could have laughed if she hadn't felt so sad. He had no idea, had he? No idea that working so near a man she loved who wasn't interested in spending his life with her was an impossibility.

'Don't be silly, Connor,' she said gently. 'I shall never forget it—but surely I don't need to spell it out. You don't believe in happy-ever-after commitment, do you? You want to keep your independence—but I'm one of these fools who, when they fall in love, want more than a casual affair.'

'It wouldn't be a casual affair,' Connor growled. 'We could—'

He was interrupted by the appearance of Pete with his ankle strapped up and two crutches to help him keep his weight off the injury. He looked much more cheerful.

'Hi. The good news is that my ankle's not broken,' he said jovially. 'And you shouldn't have waited, you two. I could easily have got a taxi.'

'Don't be silly,' said Victoria. 'We'll see you safely home. And by the way, you're going to need physio on that to keep it mobile when it's calmed down a bit, even if it's not broken.'

'That's one of the things I wanted to bring up at the next practice meeting,' remarked Connor. 'We need a weekly physio clinic at the surgery. It would save a trek to hospital for many of our patients.'

'I'll certainly support that if it helps me,' said Pete. 'I'll put forward a strong case for all the surgeries in our cluster to agree to it!'

They dropped him off at his house and Victoria made them all a cup of tea.

'Thanks both of you—I'm so grateful for your help,' said Pete. 'I feel such a fool…but don't worry, I'll be in on Monday.'

'Don't be daft. You must have a few days off to let that ankle settle,' said Connor firmly.

'I've got crutches,' protested Pete. 'And it feels better already.'

All the runners had congregated back at the field behind the surgery and the catering volunteers were doing a brisk trade in selling soft drinks, tea and buns by the time Victoria and Connor got back.

Victoria went into the building where Maggie was sorting through all the entry tickets and names of those who had run. She looked up as Victoria came in and gave a jubilant thumbs-up.

'We've raised ever so much money!' she exclaimed. 'And with the picture Mr Lamont's given for auction, we'll be way above our estimate.'

'That's marvellous,' Victoria said. She glanced at the clock above the desk. 'You buzz off home now, Maggie—you've done enough. I'll stay and put on the alarm—there's some paperwork I've got to do yet.'

'Right. See you Monday!'

Maggie went out and Victoria went to one of the filing cabinets. The day had been a bigger success than she could have imagined, except for Pete's unfortunate accident—and that funny hollow feeling that soon she would not be part of the practice any more. She extracted the file she needed, then turned round. A voice behind her said, 'Excuse me…'

A tall blonde woman was standing at the desk with a baby in her arms. Her face seemed vaguely familiar.

The woman said in businesslike tones, 'Sorry to bother you—but I wonder if Dr Connor Saunders is here? I'd like to speak to him if possible.'

'I'm afraid he's gone home. The surgery's normally closed on a Saturday afternoon. It's only been open today for the charity fun run we've had this morning. But if it's something urgent, I'm a doctor in the practice and maybe I could help. Is your baby not well?'

The woman shook her head. 'Oh, no, nothing like that. It's personal, actually. You see, I'm Carol Saunders—Connor's wife. It's very important that I see him soon. Do you have his address? I seem to have mislaid it.' She jiggled the baby up and down, smiling at the child. 'And Lucy wants to see him too, don't you, darling?'

The world stood still for a moment as Victoria stared at Carol in bewilderment.

'Connor's wife?' she faltered. 'Oh, I didn't realise that you were—'

'Living together any more?' Carol smiled as she finished Victoria's sentence. 'It's true, we did separate. But, of course, Connor was devastated when we broke up—begged me to stay and said he would always be there for me—so I know he'll be delighted I've come back. I suppose he told you about Lucy?'

'I…I'm not sure…' stammered Victoria through lips that seemed strangely paralysed. Her heart rocketed against her rib cage, and she held on to the edge of the counter very tightly. Now she knew why the woman's face was familiar. She'd seen a photograph of her in Connor's flat—their wedding photograph—only a few days before.

Her throat went very dry and she swallowed painfully. In a calm voice that she couldn't believe was her own she said to Carol, 'Well, how do you do? I'm Connor's partner in the practice, Victoria Curtis. He lives in the village main street—number eleven. I expect he'll be there by now.'

Carol gave a bright smile. 'Thank you. I'll be off, then. Con and I have a lot to discuss!' She paused for a second and turned back. 'You wouldn't do me a great favour, would you? Just ring him and tell him I'm on my way!'

She went out with the baby and Victoria heard a car start up and take off down the road. She started to tremble and sat down on a chair in front of the desk. Connor had lied to her. He'd said he was divorced, yet Carol had implied they were merely separated. He'd told her he had no children—had he forgotten he had a beautiful baby? He'd told her he had no contact with Carol—but here she was. There was something chillingly intimate in the way Carol had called Connor 'Con'—as if he really did still belong to this woman who had known him so long.

Of course, thought Victoria bleakly, all this should make no difference to her now—she was going away. But if she'd known he wasn't free, she would have kept her distance. He was just like Andy, wasn't he? Both of them had deceived her.

She picked up the phone and stabbed out Connor's home number. When he picked up the phone she said coldly, 'Victoria here. Your wife has just been to the surgery with the baby. She assumed I knew about your little girl. She's asked me to tell you she'll be round to see you in a minute. Apparently little Lucy is longing to see you.'

She slammed down the phone before Connor could answer, then marched out of the surgery, tears streaming down her face.

CHAPTER NINE

'It's Sam Tolly,' said Maggie, putting her head round the door. 'He's hurt his knee and it's very swollen. Can you see him?'

Victoria grimaced, and put aside the few applications they'd had for the locum job she'd advertised. 'OK.' She sighed. 'Has he had a bath recently, do you think?'

Maggie grinned. 'I'm afraid you'll need air freshener—I think he's been loading manure…'

Sam Tolly, local tramp and odd-job man, although of a cheerful disposition, was all she needed to make a bad day worse, thought Victoria glumly. What she really wanted was to go somewhere very quiet by herself and curl up in a miserable ball and cry for about ten hours. She'd had a sleepless night trying to get to grips with the fact that Connor had deceived her over the circumstances of his marriage, and she felt a boiling mixture of distress at his deception and fury at herself for being so naïve as to believe anything he'd said.

Today he had appeared only briefly to do his surgery and a clinic and now it was nearly noon and he would start his half-day off. He had left a note on her desk. All it said was, 'I'm coming round this evening to discuss things—Connor.'

If he thought he was coming round to see her tonight, he

had another think coming, she thought savagely. She would make sure she wasn't in all evening.

'Hello, Doc! Good of you to see me at the end of your surgery.' Sam Tolly's cheerful voice broke into her thoughts and he limped in, leaning heavily on an old stick, a strong aroma of farmyard drifting in with him.

Victoria tried to breathe as shallowly as she could. 'What have you done to yourself this time, Sam? Fallen off that ladder of yours?'

Sam chuckled. 'Not far wrong, Doc! The thing is, one of the dogs got their lead tangled round the base of the ladder and pulled me to my knees sudden like. They've swollen up like blinking barrage balloons. Can you give me something for them?'

'Sit down and I'll have a look at them.'

Victoria gestured to the chair in front of the desk and Sam lowered himself with a grunt. She made a mental note to give the seat a good clean later. Sam pulled up his filthy jeans and revealed badly swollen and puffy knees.

Victoria pursed her lips and probed them very gently, stopping when Sam winced. 'Those do look painful, Sam. I'll have to draw off some of the fluid that's collected around the joints and give you a broad-spectrum antibiotic because they look as if they're infected.'

Sam nodded. 'I knew you'd have the answer! You doctors can treat anything these days, can't you? Ruddy marvellous!'

'I don't know if we can cure all ills, Sam,' said Victoria bleakly. If only a broken heart could be healed as simply as an infected knee, she thought bitterly, going over to a cupboard and taking out a pack of syringes. What Connor had inflicted on her was going to take a long, long time to get better.

She pulled on some sterile gloves and disinfected the swollen areas of Sam's knees with swabs before putting needles in and aspirating the straw-coloured liquid that was building up around the joints.

'There—that should feel a lot better.'

Sam stood up gingerly, then walked about rather stiffly. 'Aye! That feels a lot better, Doc.' He looked at Victoria and shook his head. 'Can't say you look too chipper, mind you—you look ruddy awful! Bags under yer eyes and white as a ghost. What do they say? Physician, heal thyself, eh? About time you took yourself to a good doctor, never mind me!'

Cackling with laughter, he limped out. Victoria took her compact out of her bag and peered at herself in the mirror. He's right, she thought. I look absolutely terrible. And all thanks to Connor Saunders making a complete fool of me!

There was a tap on the door and Maggie came in again. 'Ah, just checking, Victoria. Thought you might have passed out after Sam's visit! Would you like this spray to freshen things up a bit?'

Despite herself, Victoria laughed. 'At least he's a cheerful man—and very appreciative. Not many with his sunny disposition.'

'I really came in to say that Doug Simons, the drug rep, has been here for a while. He said you had an appointment at twelve o'clock…'

Victoria clapped her hand to her forehead. 'Oh, heavens, I forgot all about him, Maggie. Where is he?'

'I put him in the mother and baby room. You all right? You sound a bit rough.'

'I'm OK. Just a bit of a headache. Send him through and I'll give him half an hour.'

Perhaps, she thought wryly, listening to Doug Simons's sales pitch on a drug to help irritable bladders would take her mind off Connor for a few minutes. Or perhaps it wouldn't…

The young sales rep came in, smiling breezily, and launched quickly into his sales pitch. Victoria tried to concentrate on what he was saying but her thoughts tended to drift off as she pondered the situation with Connor.

She came back to earth suddenly when Doug raised his voice. 'As I was saying, Dr Curtis, this new slow-release formulation means that the patient only needs to take it once a week—a most attractive attribute, I'm sure you'll agree.'

'Sounds interesting…' said Victoria cautiously.

'I'm sure when you and Dr Saunders have discussed the costings you'll find in the long run it's a very cost-effective drug,' the young man continued enthusiastically.

'Well, it's obviously more expensive than the conventional drug we've been using.'

Doug opened his mouth to expound further when a sharp rap on the door stopped him. Before Victoria could say anything the door opened and Connor strode in, grim-faced, his fair hair tousled, as if he'd just run his hands through it.

He ignored the surprised sales rep and, putting his hands on the desk, leaned towards Victoria. He said forcefully, 'You've got it all wrong, Victoria. Carol came here completely unexpectedly. I had no idea she was even in the area.'

Victoria's pulse accelerated, first in astonishment at his sudden entrance and then because he looked so damned attractive and sexy with his blue eyes ablaze with emotion. She swallowed, putting that thought to the back of her mind, and leapt to her feet, looking at him angrily.

'I'm in the middle of a meeting with Doug. I'd rather you

didn't barge in. And as for the matter of Carol, I don't believe a word you say!'

Connor looked at her fiercely. 'You will believe me. I'll explain it tonight. I would never lie to you, never!'

She bent forward over the desk so that their faces were quite close, her own eyes sparking angrily. 'I'm sick of being sweet-talked by you! And, anyway, it doesn't matter what your explanations are because I won't be here long.'

His voice was slow and deliberate. 'Victoria, I told you the truth. I haven't seen Carol for ages. I've had nothing to do with her.'

'What about the small matter of the baby?' she said scornfully. 'And the fact that you told her you'd always be there for her? I must say I can't get over your leaving Glasgow when you had a child there.'

He ran his hands through his hair in exasperation so that it stood up in peaks round his forehead. 'Oh, for God's sake, give me a break. I'll explain it tonight!'

Doug looked open mouthed from one to the other, then his gaze followed Connor as he turned on his heel and marched out of the room, closing the door none too gently behind him. Doug looked back at Victoria rather uncomfortably.

'If you'd like me to go…if it's inconvenient…' he faltered.

Connor's sudden entrance and the fury she felt with the man seemed to release a new energy in Victoria. She smiled at the discomfited rep and said soothingly, 'It's perfectly convenient, Doug. Run over those points again with me, and then we'll have the delicious sandwiches I bet you've brought with you!'

She went over to close the window against the definite nip in the air and then stopped for a second. She could see Carol standing in the car park with her baby in a buggy, probably waiting for Connor.

'I'd like to know how he's going to explain the baby's presence,' she said angrily to herself.

'I beg your pardon?' said Doug politely.

Victoria jumped. 'Nothing. Just talking to myself. Do carry on, please.'

Doug looked at her doubtfully, then unfurled a large graph. 'I'm sure you'll be interested to see the correlation between those that have had the drug and the control group who haven't,' he said.

Victoria sighed and prepared to look interested for the next quarter of an hour.

Some days were longer than others—this had been rather a marathon, and sitting down that evening in front of a roaring fire, with Buttons lying comfortably on her feet, Victoria felt absolutely exhausted, mentally and physically. She was immeasurably sad. It felt as if she'd had a rerun of her time with Andy. Both he and Connor had deceived her, and although Connor had never promised her any future with him, he had given the impression that he was a single man again with no responsibilities. She didn't want to hear his explanation about Carol and the baby's presence in Braithwaite. How thin was the dividing line between love and hate? she thought. At the moment she felt that she despised Connor for misleading her.

She leant forward and poked the fire, sending a blaze of flame up the chimney. Emotionally she wasn't up to seeing Connor, and somehow she would have to find the energy to go out that evening before he appeared, as he'd threatened.

She sighed as she stroked the dog. 'I don't know, Buttons. When it comes to men I've no judgement at all...'

Buttons thumped his tail sleepily, then suddenly sat up and gave a sharp bark as the doorbell rang. Victoria sprang up from the sofa, slightly panic-stricken. She hadn't expected Connor to arrive so early, and now here he was and she couldn't bear to listen to his explanations.

The bell rang again and she snatched the front door open. 'I told you not to come round,' she snapped aggressively, then stopped in embarrassment. Pete was standing in front of her, supported by two crutches under his arms.

'Pete! I...I'm sorry. I thought you were someone else. Er...do come in. How is your ankle? Surely you shouldn't be up on it so soon?'

He smiled sheepishly. 'It's a lot better now I've had it strapped up and got my weight off it,' he said, hopping in on his one good foot. 'The thing is, look, this is probably right out of order, just a spur-of-the-moment thing, but I was going to this concert tonight and I wondered if you'd like to come with me. Bit late notice, I'm afraid, but I was damned if I was going to miss it because of my leg.'

'That's very kind of you,' said Victoria in surprise. Although she and Pete saw each other frequently at work, they didn't really socialise. When she'd taken him home after his accident it had been the first time she'd been to his house.

'A bit cheeky really.' He smiled. 'My brother was coming with me but he's got held up at work. I hope you don't mind my asking.'

'Not at all...' Victoria gave the suggestion quick consideration. If she went with Pete she'd be out when Connor

ame. She smiled cheerfully at him. 'Sure, I'd love to come.
Wait there and I'll just get a coat.'

A few seconds later and they were walking slowly down
he drive, Pete doing his best with his crutches.

'Luckily I've got an automatic,' he was saying, 'otherwise
'd be really stuck.'

A pair of headlights swung into the drive and a car parked
ust beyond them. Connor leapt out, then stopped in surprise
s Victoria and Pete passed him.

'Hi, Connor!' Pete called out. 'Have you left something at
he surgery?'

'No…I was coming to speak to Victoria about something,'
e began, staring at them both.

'I'm going out to a concert with Pete,' said Victoria lightly.
'I'm afraid it's not convenient.' She turned to Pete. 'Shall I
drive? It might be easier.'

'Thanks. That would be great. We'll take the York road.'
Pete tossed her the keys, then turned cheerily back to the
ilent Connor. 'See you tomorrow, then!'

As she drove off, Victoria flicked a glance in her rear-view
mirror and could see Connor standing looking after them under
he light of the streetlamp by the drive. He looked very sombre.

'I hope Connor didn't have anything important to discuss,'
aid Pete. 'He seemed a little taken aback.'

'Oh, no,' said Victoria brightly. 'I'm sure it was of no con-
equence at all.' She accelerated out of a corner rather hard,
scattering stones, and Pete glanced at her nervously. 'No con-
equence at all,' she repeated firmly.

Connor watched Victoria and Pete drive off with a feeling of
rustration. He was never going to persuade Victoria that it

was all over between him and Carol. It was true that he had always told his wife that he wanted the marriage to work, even when they'd been at their unhappiest together, but then she'd left him for someone else. She cared no more for his feeling than if he'd been some hired help she'd no longer needed, he thought bitterly. Typical of her that when things hadn't worked out quite as she'd envisaged, she should want to return to the safe haven of her ex-husband.

Connor kicked a stone angrily across the path and got back into his car. He sat for a moment, his hands gripping the steering-wheel, trying to marshal his thoughts. He hadn't wanted to work with Victoria at first—she had a feisty manner which reminded him too much of the controlling Carol—but gradually he'd begun to realise that she was nothing like Carol at all. OK, she knew her own mind, but she wasn't a control freak. He gazed bleakly into the dark night and sighed. Victoria had meant it when she'd said she was leaving, and it was becoming clearer every minute that he couldn't envisage a life without her.

Angrily he turned the key in the ignition and somehow he wasn't surprised when the car wouldn't start—a fitting end to a miserable day. He scowled. He leapt out of the car and opened the bonnet, peering into the engine with his pocket torch as the rain poured down on him, running in rivulets down his face. As he fiddled with a lead that had come out of its socket he determined on one thing—he wouldn't let Victoria go without a struggle. Dammit, he thought as he slammed the bonnet shut, he needed her, didn't seem able to function without her. Suddenly, keeping his independence didn't seem such a good idea.

* * *

Victoria tried to enjoy the concert. Pete was pleasant company, if rather dull, but her sadness about Connor kept coming over her in waves. Afterwards Pete insisted on taking her to a little Italian restaurant and they had pizzas and ice cream. He told her about his childhood, growing up with his brother on a poor estate in Liverpool, and how, to his parents' pride, he had managed to get a place at university.

'And did you enjoy it?' asked Victoria.

He shrugged. 'I didn't fit in very well—I've always been a bit awkward socially. The Billy Bunter of the class, I suppose.' He looked a bit embarrassed, as if he'd confessed something terrible. 'I shouldn't be eating this stuff really. I'm supposed to be cutting down.'

Victoria smiled. 'You can start tomorrow,' she suggested.

It was still quite early when they arrived back at The Cedars, but Victoria felt too tired to ask Pete in for a coffee.

'Thank you so much. I've really enjoyed the evening,' she said as she opened the car door. 'Are you all right to drive the car yourself now?'

'Oh, yes, no problem.' He looked at her rather awkwardly. 'I've enjoyed this evening as well. You wouldn't think of doing this sort of thing again…perhaps the cinema next time?' he asked hesitantly.

A flicker of embarrassment went through Victoria. She certainly hadn't thought of this outing as being the start of something regular, and she wasn't going to divulge that she was leaving soon anyway.

'That would great some time.' She smiled. Then she added with some truth, 'I've got to sort out where I'm going to live permanently in the next few weeks, of course…'

'Oh, yes. Your mother is coming back soon, isn't she?

Well, as soon as you're sorted we'll make another evening of it. Anyway, see you tomorrow at the practice meeting!'

Pete drove off with a happy wave and Victoria was stricken with remorse that she might have given Pete the wrong idea. He was a nice man, but she would never be able to think of him in a romantic way, and she had a feeling that given any encouragement he would be keen to put their relationship on a permanent footing. Why do I always fall for the wrong kind of men? she wondered sadly.

She let herself into the house and was struck by another thought. She would have to confront Connor tomorrow at the practice meeting—and how difficult would that be?

Victoria sat as far away as she could from Connor at the other end of the table, and looked fixedly down at the agenda for the meeting. She was supremely aware of him there—almost as if they had been sitting next to each other. She knew that those blue eyes of his were gazing at her intently, and it was with an effort that she turned to Pete with as natural smile as she could muster.

'Lovely evening last night. I enjoyed that concert!'

'I'm so pleased. It was great, wasn't it?'

'Can we hurry up and start this meeting?' said Connor in a rasping voice, tapping his fingers impatiently on the table and glowering at them. 'We've all got things to do.'

Maggie, taking the minutes, and Karen looked at him, slightly surprised at his irritable manner. Recently Connor had been relaxed and even-tempered. Victoria flicked a look at him. His expression was dour, unsmiling.

'Right, first off we're discussing the provision for home visits to the housebound on a regular basis and then the new phlebotomy nurse,' said Pete. 'Karen and a team of nurses from other practices in the area are organising a rota for visits, which, of course, will be quite expensive—'

'But could save money in the long run if we catch small problems before they become major ones,' put in Karen.

The agenda was a full one and there were lively discussions, although Connor was uncharacteristically quiet, only commenting fairly forcibly on the desirability of a physiotherapy clinic to be held at least once a fortnight at the surgery.

'That's going to eat into the funds,' commented Victoria. 'St Hilda's isn't all that far away—in fact, it's virtually in the town centre. We could do with the money for more vital things perhaps.'

'Such as?' said Connor tersely. 'The hospital covers most things, but the more we can provide here, the more complete our service. Surely you can see that?'

When he was angry, thought Victoria bleakly, looking at his glowering expression, Connor exuded a powerful sexuality. His blue eyes seemed to darken and his good-looking face had a strong, unyielding appearance. That was the thing about Connor—he could look very tough but she would never have believed that he would be dishonest. Quick-tempered, impatient perhaps, but not dishonest. Part of her longed to know just why Carol had come to see him. Had he known about the baby or had it been a total surprise? Then Victoria thought sadly that it didn't really matter what the explanation was—she would be leaving soon anyway.

Maggie brought in some coffee and biscuits and Victoria poured herself a strong cup and listened to Karen explaining about a new bandage that had been produced for helping in the treatment of intractable ulcers. Connor didn't join in the discussion—he was watching Victoria. He thought with a pang how utterly gorgeous she looked, her thick hair held back by an Alice band and hanging like a sheet of shining silk almost to her shoulders, a shaft of light through the window making its auburn highlights gleam. When she turned her head it swung sleekly back and forth and he could almost feel its silky texture when he looked at it. Had it only been a few days ago that she had been in his arms and they had made love so passionately, and he had buried his face in that sweet-smelling hair? Now it was as if they were strangers who had barely met each other.

He groaned inwardly. Trust Carol to come back and mess his life up just when he'd begun to realise that Victoria meant much more to him than he'd ever thought. Everything seemed to be falling apart like a house of cards, and all because of a selfish woman who didn't care how many lives she ruined.

He stared unseeingly before him and gripped the pencil he was holding so hard that it snapped with a crack.

Victoria looked across at him and for a moment their eyes met in mutual misery. Connor got up abruptly, scraping his chair back, and said tersely, 'I must go—I've a patient to see at St Hilda's.'

As he passed behind Victoria, the back of his hand brushed briefly against the nape of her neck. She froze for a second as she felt its warmth and remembered how that same hand had caressed her body so passionately a few days ago. No doubt about it—she must get a locum as soon as possible and put distance between her and Connor.

CHAPTER TEN

SUDDENLY the weather had become very cold. Victoria wrapped her coat closely round her as she crossed the yard to the surgery and glanced up at the leaden sky. Even the weather seems to fit in with how I feel, she thought sadly. The practice meeting the day before had been excruciating and she'd felt the atmosphere between her and Connor could have been cut with a knife.

Connor had pushed a note through her letterbox that morning, which had been terse and to the point.

'I need to speak to you soon about the date you plan to leave and the provision of a locum. We can't continue like this. I'll see you after work today—C.'

She went through Reception and waved at Maggie and Lucy. 'I'll go straight into my room,' she called out.

'Coffee?' enquired Maggie.

'That would be great—thank you.'

Maggie followed her in and put down the cup of hot liquid. She looked at Victoria thoughtfully. 'Are you sure you're all right?' she said with concern. 'You didn't look too good at the meeting yesterday.'

Victoria swallowed hard and gave a humourless laugh.

'Just a personal matter really—something I have to work through myself, Maggie. I'll be fine—honestly.'

'Well…if I can be of any help, you know where I am,' said Maggie kindly.

Did Maggie have an inkling about what was going on? Victoria shrugged and thought that at least it was good to know that she had some support. She took a deep breath and pressed the button for the first patient. In a few seconds little Harry Tate trotted in with his very pregnant mother, Jane.

'Hello again, Harry,' said Victoria, bending down to the five-year-old's level. 'Why aren't you wearing your Superman outfit?'

Harry smiled a gap-toothed grin. 'Mummy put it in the washing-machine and it's come out all black—and so has everything else!'

Victoria laughed. The little boy had such an impish look that even the gloom she felt over Connor lifted a bit. 'Oh, dear—that's so easy to do, though!'

'His father wasn't too pleased when all his football shorts turned a nice shade of grey, I can tell you! I think this pregnancy is robbing me of my brain—I'm always doing silly things.' Jane flopped down on the chair in front of the desk and puffed out her cheeks tiredly.

'Well, not much longer till D-day, is it? You've come in for your check-up so let me see what your blood pressure is. How are you feeling?'

'Utterly exhausted! I keep getting these pains. I think they're contractions, but after a while they subside. It's made me a bit nervous that the baby's on the way and I won't be able to get to hospital. Harry arrived in quite a rush.'

Victoria gave her a reassuring smile. 'I shouldn't worry at

all. I'm sure you'll have plenty of time to get there! And I don't think anything will happen yet awhile—you're still three weeks off. I'll do a blood test just to establish if you're a bit iron deficient. I'm pretty confident that the contractions you're feeling are Braxton Hicks' contractions—the uterus contracting in preparation for the birth. Did you not have them with Harry?'

'Perhaps I did, but I wasn't so aware of them, and it was a few years ago now.'

'Right. Well, I'll just let Harry look in the play box while you get up on the bed. We'll see if the baby's head's dropped down yet.'

Jane waddled over to the bed, then just as she was about to heave herself up with Victoria's assistance, she stopped and gave a sudden muffled cry.

'Oh, my God…I don't believe it!' she croaked.

Victoria looked at her enquiringly. 'You OK?'

Jane's eyes were wide with horror and shock. 'It's my waters,' she whispered. 'They've broken. It's all over the place. What a mess!'

Both women stared at the large pool of water that Jane was standing in. It was getting bigger by the second. Little Harry was still absorbed in playing with the cars in the toy box and hadn't noticed anything amiss. Then Jane gave a sharp intake of breath and bent forward, clutching her stomach with one hand and Victoria's hand with the other.

'Ahh! The pain! I'm sure this isn't a Braxton whatsit! I've started labour!'

'So much for my reassurances,' remarked Victoria wryly, her heart hammering almost as much as Jane's was. 'Now,' she said with a calmness that hid the panic she was feeling inside at the thought of delivering a baby in the surgery, 'up you get on that bed. I'm going to call an ambulance because you need to be in hospital now your waters have broken.'

Jane gave another groan and gripped Victoria's hand even harder, then after a few seconds, when the pain had subsided, she said with slight hysteria, 'That's another one. I'm getting these contractions pretty close together, aren't I?'

Victoria glanced across at Harry, who was looking up at his mother with fright, his lips trembling ominously.

'It's all right, Harry,' she said quickly. 'Mummy's fine. I'm going to give her some medicine in a minute, but first you come with me, and Maggie will take you to see the ducks in the pond at the back. Won't that be nice?'

She took the little boy's hand firmly and took him out, stopping at the door to say to Jane, 'Just hang on in there. I'll be back in one minute when I've taken Harry to Maggie.'

'Don't be long,' implored Jane hoarsely.

Maggie was leaning forward, talking to an elderly patient, but Victoria pushed Harry in front of her. 'Sorry about barging in—we've a bit of an emergency. If you'd give us a minute?'

'Oh, dear,' said the old lady. 'I'll go and sit down, then— let you get on with it!'

'What's up?' asked Maggie in surprise.

'I need you to take Harry out to see the ducks.' She glanced at the little boy, who was gazing up at her solemnly, and dropped her voice. 'His mum's gone into labour and I don't know how long we've got.'

'Of course. Lucy can take over from me,' said Maggie, cottoning on to the situation quickly and coming round the counter with a smile for the little boy. 'Shall we take some bread for those hungry ducks, lovey? And perhaps you'd like a biscuit and a drink of milk out there as well?'

'When can I see Mummy?' he asked.

'Very soon, love. She'll stay here as she's a bit tired while we feed these ducks—OK?'

Harry seemed to accept that explanation, trotting off happily enough with Maggie, and Victoria lifted the phone.

'Let me ring for an ambulance while you get back to Jane,' said a deep voice before she could start dialling.

Connor was standing behind her and she whipped round with relief in her eyes. She forgot about hating him, not wanting to have anything to do with him any more. All she could think about at that moment was Jane about to produce a baby in the surgery and needing help. The sight of Connor standing there was the most reassuring thing in the world at that precise moment.

'Yes!' she said urgently. 'And then, please, come in and help—it's been a long time since I've delivered a baby and if the ambulance doesn't come quickly, I think it's going to make its appearance in my room!'

'No worries. I'll get the emergency delivery pack out of the cupboard. It might be an idea to try and get hold of her husband as well—we've probably got his phone number on our files.'

Karen came out of one of the treatment rooms, where she'd been giving injections, and looked enquiringly as Victoria dashed past her and back to her room.

'Karen! I think we'll need you. Jane Tate's gone into labour and the contractions are pretty close. First, can you explain to the other patients that there may be a delay in seeing them?'

Karen looked startled, then grinned. 'That's exciting. I'll be right back!'

* * *

Jane was tossing and turning on the bed and turned a fright-ened face towards Victoria.

'I know it's coming! I can feel it pressing down, I'm sure. What about Harry? Is he all right?'

'He's absolutely fine, Jane. He's gone to feed the ducks with Maggie—don't worry. And Dr Saunders is getting hold of your husband.'

Karen slipped into the room and Victoria looked at her gratefully. 'Can you help Jane off with some of those clothes and put some clean towels under her?' she asked. 'Then we can look and see what's happening to this baby and how near he or she is to being born.'

Connor appeared and closed the door behind him. 'How are we doing?' he asked.

Jane screwed up her face again and arched her back as she gave a yell of pain. 'I'm having another contraction. Oh, my God…it's terrible. Help me, please!'

Victoria took Jane's hand. 'You're all right, Jane,' she said calmly. 'Grip my hand as tightly as you can. You're doing so well. I'd say the contractions are coming every couple of minutes. This baby's certainly in a hurry.' She flicked a look across at Connor and Karen and murmured, 'I don't think he's going to wait for the ambulance to arrive. Connor, have you got that small foetal Doppler machine? Let's have a listen to the heartbeat when this contraction's over.'

He passed her the machine and some lubricating jelly, which she smeared over Jane's swollen stomach, then she passed the machine over the bump. A sound almost like little feet patter-ing rhythmically along the ground floated into the room and even Jane smiled at the sound of her baby's heartbeat.

'Sounds nice and strong and regular,' remarked Connor as he

vashed his hands and put on some gloves. He glanced at Victoria.
OK if I examine Jane and see how things are progressing?'

Victoria nodded, reflecting wryly that when they'd started
vorking together he might not have bothered to ask her.

After a few seconds he straightened up and said with a
mile, 'It's all systems go. I can see the crown of your baby's
ead—he or she has fair hair! You're doing marvellously,
ane. Everything's going normally, so don't worry. You've
one nearly all the hard work.'

Victoria flicked a look at Connor. He was so calm, smiling
own at Jane to encourage her, giving the woman confidence
hat all was well, even though they were in a completely alien
lace to the maternity unit she should have been in. Jane even
nanaged to smile at them before she clutched Victoria's hand
gain and shrieked loudly as the baby's regular heartbeat
uddenly became faster.

'Here's another one… I want to push. The baby's coming
ow, I know! Ahh!'

Karen held the woman's other hand and Connor said calmly,
Now we want you to pant for a minute. Only push when we
ay so! You're doing so well, Jane… Now, push. Come on!'

They all chorused, 'Well done! That's brilliant!' as the
ead appeared for a second, and then, after another push,
ame further down the birth canal. Jane was concentrating
ow on getting her baby into the world, trying to do what the
octors and Karen were exhorting her to do, putting her chin
o her chest and pushing as hard as she could.

Suddenly there was a slippery, gushing noise and a final
roan from Jane, and a little body slithered into Connor's
vaiting hands. He held the baby up and looked at it tenderly.

'Welcome, little one,' he said softly. Then he looked at

Jane with a beaming smile. 'Congratulations Jane. You've got a beautiful little girl.'

As if in answer, the little girl opened her mouth and gave a loud yell, her crumpled face becoming pink as she breathed in oxygen and it flooded through her body.

Victoria and Karen looked at each other with tears running down their faces and gave whoops of delight. 'You clever girl Jane. Oh, look at the little treasure—isn't she gorgeous?'

'She's got a good pair of lungs on her!' remarked Connor as Victoria cut and clamped the umbilical cord.

She looked up for a second at Connor, and saw to her surprise that there were tears in his eyes as well. Then their eyes met and like the leap of electricity between two wires there was sudden empathy between them, a rush of mutual relief that all was well after the drama of the past few minutes. The expression in his dark-lashed eyes deepened.

'A good bit of teamwork there,' he murmured, then he handed the baby gently to Karen, who wrapped her in a blanket.

Victoria pushed thoughts of Connor away and turned to the happy mother. 'What are you going to call her, Jane?'

Jane lay back on the bed and smiled a beatific smile at them all. 'Victoria Karen, of course. I might even add Connor as third name! She's just what we wanted. Thank you…thank you all so much!'

They all laughed and Victoria said, 'That's a fantastic honour. I hope the practice will be looking after her for many years to come.' She started to press Jane's stomach. 'Just trying to encourage the afterbirth to come,' she said. 'Then you can hold your little girl.'

Karen gave the baby to Jane after the afterbirth had been

delivered and then went to get the baby scales from the mother and baby room.

'And I'll tell everyone the happy news!' she declared.

She ran out and a second later the sound of a huge cheer floated through to the makeshift delivery room.

'Hear that?' Connor grinned. 'Your daughter's a little star!'

In another few minutes, after Karen had appeared with the scales and a cup of tea for Jane, there was the sound of an ambulance siren coming down the road.

'Better late than never,' said Karen. 'Shall I go and get little Harry to come and see his new sister?'

There was the sound of footsteps running down the corridor and the door burst open.

'I haven't missed the birth, have I?'

Jane looked across at the man standing in the doorway and started to laugh. 'I'm sorry, John, our daughter was a bit early…'

John gave a whoop of delight. 'A girl?' he yelled, then came over to the bed and hugged Jane. 'Thank you, darling,' they heard him murmur. 'Thank you for our little girl. What a miracle!' Then he turned to the other three. 'She's the first female in our family not to be late, then,' he said with a smile, and took the baby from his wife, looking down at the child with wonder and pride.

Mother and baby had been taken in the ambulance, and John had followed with Harry. Connor and Victoria were left alone in her room, he at one side, she at the other. They stood staring at each other for a long moment, still united by the excitement and adrenalin of helping a patient give birth.

'Quite a morning,' he said quietly. 'But a very happy one.'

'Yes, very happy. I…I'm glad you were there to help,' she said rather breathlessly. 'To be honest, it's nice to have back-up.'

'Even from me?' he asked wryly. He pulled off the gloves he'd been wearing and tossed them in the bin. 'To be honest, I wouldn't have missed it—it's one of the happier events in medicine, helping at the birth of a healthy child. Beats dealing with some of the patients we see.'

Victoria's mood changed to something like despair. How could she not love someone who was so moved by the birth of a child? He had shown so much care and compassion in the last half-hour, and it was hard to believe that such a man would deceive her. She bit her lip and then took a deep breath.

'Why did you lie to me, Connor?'

He looked at her steadily. 'I didn't lie. I told you, I've not seen Carol for months and months—since our divorce.'

'She said she was your wife…that you had said you'd always be there for her.'

Connor looked at her calmly. 'She was my wife—she isn't now. And, yes, I believe in marriage—I wanted to make it work. But she left me. She divorced me and went to someone else.'

A picture of Carol with the baby in her arms floated into Victoria's mind. Her voice broke. 'I don't know what to believe,' she whispered.

Connor strode across the room and looked down at Victoria intently with his piercing blue eyes. 'Haven't you learned anything about me during these past weeks? If you can't trust me now, then it's right we should part.'

He bunched his hands in his pockets and continued in a low voice, 'You don't know Carol and yet you believed what she said, or rather jumped to conclusions. You know me so much better, but you condemned me without a hearing.'

'What was I supposed to think?'

'You could have asked me first, instead of assuming the worst about me. You don't know all my background—but that doesn't mean I'd betray you, like Andy did.'

He put his hands on her shoulders, and it felt as if an electric shock had flashed through her body at their touch. It was almost as it had been a few days ago, she thought sadly. He was so close to her she could see the dark flecks in his eyes, the slightest stubble he'd missed when he'd shaved. But, of course, this time they weren't about to make love…

'Victoria, don't leave…please.' His voice was urgent and he was looking down at her intently. 'I want you to stay here… I need you. Don't go.'

There was almost a palpable silence in the room after he'd finished speaking, then Maggie's voice floating over the intercom. 'Sorry to disturb you, folks, but there's a room full of people here, all wanting to unload their worries onto you.'

Connor went out of the room and closed the door quietly behind him.

Victoria did not know how she got through the day. When Connor had finished speaking she knew with certainty that she still loved him and would have given anything to say that, whatever he'd been keeping from her, she still wanted him. But he had a child and, even though they were divorced, an ex-wife who wanted to start again.

She shut down the computer and slowly began to put on her warm coat.

With sudden resolution she picked up her bag and left the room. She couldn't leave the situation like this. She had to find out from Connor just why he'd never mentioned his child. She couldn't go through life not knowing what the whole story was. She strode out of the building with renewed purpose, waving goodbye to the girls at the desk. She would ring Connor and say she wanted to talk to him, to at least try and understand what had happened.

It had begun to snow a little as she started to cross the courtyard, and the cars that were still parked there had a coating of white. Two people were standing by Connor's car—one was Connor and it wasn't until she'd got closer that Victoria realised that the other one was Carol. Carol's voice was quite loud, and clear—easily audible to Victoria as she hesitated by the wall of the surgery before she crossed to the house.

'You can't leave me in this predicament, Connor. I have a child and I need your support!' She was shouting. 'Maybe I've been at fault as well, but remember you did promise once to love me for life!'

Connor's reply was so quiet that Victoria couldn't hear him, but she saw him open the car door and watched as they both got in the car and he drove off.

It was as if a stone had settled in her heart. Carol was right—Connor did have a duty to support her and their child, even if they were divorced. He was, of course, free to marry again now—but a child would and always should be his first priority, not his relationship with another woman. It would be unfair to expect him to make a life in Braithwaite when he should be near his daughter in Glasgow.

Bang goes my idea of having a cosy chat with Connor, she thought bleakly as she opened her front door.

The answering-machine light was blinking to show that she had a message on it. She pressed the button to hear the recording.

'Darling,' said her mother's voice brightly, 'John and I will be home at the end of the week. We're longing to see you both and hear how you've been coping with the practice. I hope it's been fun! I'll ring again tomorrow with more details of our arrival time.'

Victoria almost laughed at the inappropriate words. 'It's hardly fun at the moment, Mum,' she murmured. Then she sank down on the sofa and let the tears she'd been holding back so long flow down her cheeks. It should be a happy homecoming for her mother. Instead, it looked as if it would be a bleak and cheerless daughter who would meet Betty at the airport.

She was crying so hard she didn't hear the front door bell. It was only Buttons's furious barking that alerted her to the fact that there was someone at the door. She dabbed her eyes with her handkerchief and debated whether to bother answering it or not, but Buttons wouldn't stop flinging himself at the door and whoever it was continued to press the bell.

'All right, all right, I'm coming…' she shouted, hauling herself up out of the sofa and looking at herself in the mirror. She looked terrible—eyes swollen and red, cheeks blotched with tears. Whoever was calling would get a shock when they saw her, she thought resignedly as she undid the lock.

She opened the door and found herself staring at Connor's tall figure in the entrance. He looked at her tearful face silently for a second, then he said gently, 'Let me come in, Victoria. I need to talk to you. I'm not giving up on you without a struggle.'

She stood rooted to the spot, stunned that the man she'd been crying over a few minutes ago, the man she admitted she still loved despite anything he'd done, should be standing in front of her.

'What…what have you come back here for, Connor?' she asked stiffly. 'I saw you and Carol leave together after work and—'

He smiled grimly. 'And you heard her talking to—or rather shouting at—me?' he interrupted harshly. As if charged by a sudden impatient energy, he strode forward and pulled her towards him, looking down at her intently. 'I'm fed up with pussyfooting around, sweetheart. Just because my ex-wife has decided that I am a better bet than the father of her child and wants to come back to me, why should our lives be ruined?'

Victoria shook her head rather dazedly. 'What do you mean…the father of her child? I thought *you* were Lucy's father.'

'Just shows how you shouldn't jump to conclusions,' said Connor, pulling her down beside him on the sofa. 'Look, I didn't go into the reasons why Carol and I split up—I thought it was all water under the bridge and I wanted to move on from there.' He hesitated for a moment, as if trying to find the right words. 'I should have been more open with you from the first.'

'Then why weren't you?' asked Victoria spiritedly.

He smiled wryly and tilted her face up to his. 'Because I didn't realise that I was going to fall in love with you, and the baggage from my past seemed irrelevant.'

'So who is the little girl's father?'

Connor's hand stroked a stray piece of hair from Victoria's forehead. 'He was Carol's boss from work. She very soon became disillusioned with our marriage and the hours I kept as a GP. She thought the life of a doctor's wife would be interesting, but instead she found herself married to someone who didn't want to go out every evening after work and was loath to go with her to all the business functions she loved.'

'So that broke up the marriage?'

He shook his head and gave a twisted little smile. 'I'd say the fact that she didn't want babies was the final cause. You see, the irony is that I was longing for children...'

Victoria bit her lip. 'I thought it might be the other way round from what you told me—that you weren't too keen on the idea.'

He shook his head. 'Oh, no. Carol was set on a glittering career in the media and nothing was going to stop her—certainly not getting pregnant.'

'And yet she became pregnant with this new man?'

'She became infatuated with him—he was very successful and powerful—and, of course, that's very sexy. She believed that if she became pregnant he would leave his wife—he had no children. But she was wrong. He didn't want to break up his marriage.'

Victoria shook her head in disbelief. 'So she had a child to try and trap him? What a fool...and then she came back to you because you said you'd always be there for her.'

Connor's laugh was humourless. 'When she said she was leaving me it was a shock—I didn't know she was pregnant with his child. To be honest, we didn't have a happy marriage, so perhaps it shouldn't have been such a surprise. We led very different lives, often only meeting up late at night. Some of it was my fault, no doubt, but Carol loves her own way and, as you know, so do I!' He looked sadly at Victoria. 'But the end of a marriage is a confession of failure.'

Yes, Victoria thought. I can sympathise with that feeling of loss, regret and even anger.

'I know all about that,' she said bleakly.

'When I found out that she'd been unfaithful, that finished everything—my life with her was over.' He looked down at

Victoria and put his arms around her. 'And anyway,' he said softly, 'now it's too late.'

'Wh-what do you mean?' A little flicker of excitement started somewhere in the region of Victoria's stomach, a slight premonition that something momentous was going to happen.

'I mean it's too late for Carol to come back.' Connor's finger stroked Victoria's soft cheek and then traced a line down her neck. 'You see, I've found someone I want to be with for the rest of my life.'

Victoria stared at him breathlessly. 'You'll have to be clearer than that, Connor,' she whispered.

He smiled. 'I used to think that after my divorce I would never tie myself down again—freedom seemed a wonderful thing. Now I've begun to realise that freedom is no good unless you can do what you want with the person you love.' He turned her towards him, holding her face in his hands. 'I don't want to spend my life being independent, dammit. I want you by my side, Victoria.'

Victoria twisted away from him, her heart thumping painfully. 'What's brought this on? A week ago it seemed to me you just wanted a bit of fun, a casual affair—no commitment. What's changed your mind?'

He threw back his head and laughed. 'Sweetheart, after you'd seduced me the other night…'

She looked at him indignantly. 'You didn't need much persuasion!'

Connor gazed down at her gravely. 'What man would? I only know that in the morning I began to realise what it would mean if you left and I never saw you again. I saw a horribly bleak future. It was as if everything suddenly came into focus. And when I saw you going out with Pete I felt a rage of jealousy. I knew then, my beautiful darling, that I wanted to marry you.'

He paused for a moment and Victoria saw bright tears in his eyes. 'I've been a fool,' he said, 'but now we both have a chance of happiness. Don't let's throw it away. It may never come again.'

She stared up at his amazing blue eyes and her heart somersaulted with the beginning of a tremendous happiness.

She said with a sort of hiccupping sob, 'Oh, Connor, I do love you so much. I was a fool not to let you explain, and just assumed that Lucy was your child.' She gave a shaky laugh. 'I'm afraid my experience with Andy made me very vulnerable. I should have trusted you more.'

His eyes danced at her. 'You agree, then, that you've been a little harsh with me?'

She nodded. 'I suppose I have.'

A tender smile softened his firm mouth. 'So will you marry me, Freckles?'

And a laugh bubbled up from deep within her. 'As soon as you like, Connor.'

Their eyes mirrored their happiness as they gazed at each other, and a picture of the young brash Connor at the sixth form dance flickered into Victoria's mind.

'What a long way we've come, Connor,' she whispered as her arms wound round his neck.

Connor began to undress her slowly. 'Then let's celebrate a happy ending,' he said softly. 'Now we've got things straightened out, let's relax a little, shall we?'

And she smiled as he gazed at her naked body before him and held out her hand to lead him to the bedroom. 'We'll start again,' she said.

*   *   *

The airport was jammed with people waiting at the barrier fo
the returning passengers. Victoria peered through the crowd
trying to pick out Betty and John.

'There they are!' she cried. 'And, my, don't they look tanned?'

She and Connor rushed forward to greet them and there
were hugs and laughter all round.

Betty stood back for a moment and looked at her daughte
enquiringly. 'So have you two managed to keep the practice
going?' she asked. 'No great falling-out between you? I didn'
get the impression either of you were very keen to work with
the other to start with!'

'I dare say they managed very well without us,' put in
John. 'They both look amazingly well.' He smiled at them. '
don't suppose anything momentous has happened since we've
been away?'

Victoria and Connor looked at each other and laughed
'You're never going to believe this,' Victoria said, 'but we do
have something to tell you…'

MILLS & BOON®

MEDICAL™

proudly presents

Brides of Penhally Bay

A pulse-raising collection of emotional,
tempting romances and heart-warming stories by
bestselling Mills & Boon® Medical™ authors

July 2008
Virgin Midwife, Playboy Doctor
by Margaret McDonagh

Gorgeous playboy Dr Oliver Fawkner is causing a stir...
But Oliver is only interested in getting to know
midwife Chloe MacKinnon.

August 2008
Their Miracle Baby
by Caroline Anderson

Can an accident renew Mike and Fran Trevellyan's intimacy –
and lead to the family they've always longed for?

September 2008
Sheikh Surgeon Claims His Bride
by Josie Metcalfe

Could Emily Livingston be the woman to show formidable
surgeon Zayed Khalil how to live and love again?

*Let us whisk you away to an idyllic Cornish town –
a place where hearts are made whole*

COLLECT ALL 12 BOOKS!

Available at WHSmith, Tesco, ASDA, and all good bookshops
www.millsandboon.co.uk

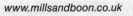

Celebrate 100 years of pure reading pleasure with Mills & Boon®

To mark our centenary, each month we're publishing a special 100th Birthday Edition. These celebratory editions are packed with extra features and include a FREE bonus story.

Plus, you have the chance to enter a fabulous monthly prize draw. See 100th Birthday Edition books for details.

Now that's worth celebrating!

July 2008

**The Man Who Had Everything
by Christine Rimmer**
Includes FREE bonus story *Marrying Molly*

August 2008

Their Miracle Baby by Caroline Anderson
Includes FREE bonus story *Making Memories*

September 2008

Crazy About Her Spanish Boss by Rebecca Winters
Includes FREE bonus story
Rafael's Convenient Proposal

Look for Mills & Boon® 100th Birthday Editions at your favourite bookseller or visit
www.millsandboon.co.uk

FREE

4 BOOKS AND A SURPRISE GIFT!

We would like to take this opportunity to thank you for reading this Mills & Boon® book by offering you the chance to take FOUR more specially selected titles from the Medical™ series absolutely FREE! We're also making this offer to introduce you to the benefits of the Mills & Boon® Book Club™—

- ★ **FREE home delivery**
- ★ **FREE gifts and competitions**
- ★ **FREE monthly Newsletter**
- ★ **Books available before they're in the shops**
- ★ **Exclusive Mills & Boon Book Club offers**

Accepting these FREE books and gift places you under no obligation to buy; you may cancel at any time, even after receiving your free shipment. Simply complete your details below and return the entire page to the address below. You don't even need a stamp!

YES! Please send me 4 free Medical books and a surprise gift. I understand that unless you hear from me, I will receive 6 superb new titles every month for just £2.99 each, postage and packing free. I am under no obligation to purchase any books and may cancel my subscription at any time. The free books and gift will be mine to keep in any case.

M8ZEE

Ms/Mrs/Miss/Mr..Initials ....

BLOCK CAPITALS PLEASE

Surname ....

Address ....

....

....Postcode ....

Send this whole page to:
The Mills & Boon Book Club, FREEPOST CN81, Croydon, CR9 3WZ

Offer valid in UK only and is not available to current Mills & Boon® Book Club™subscribers to this series. Overseas and Eire please write for details. We reserve the right to refuse an application and applicants must be aged 18 years or over. Only one application per household. Terms and prices subject to change without notice. Offer expires 31st October 2008. As a result of this application, you may receive offers from Harlequin Mills & Boon and other carefully selected companies. If you would prefer not to share in this opportunity please write to The Data Manager at PO Box 676, Richmond, TW9 1WU.

Mills & Boon® is a registered trademark owned by Harlequin Mills & Boon Limited.
Medical™ is being used as a trademark. The Mills & Boon® Book Club™ is being used as a trademark.